Cathy Williams

———

At Her Boss's Pleasure

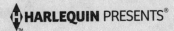

If you purchased this book without a cover you should be aware that this book is stolen property. It was reported as "unsold and destroyed" to the publisher, and neither the author nor the publisher has received any payment for this "stripped book."

ISBN-13: 978-0-373-13817-3

At Her Boss's Pleasure

First North American Publication 2015

Copyright © 2015 by Cathy Williams

PLEASE RECYCLE · THIS PRODUCT IS RECYCLABLE ·

Recycling programs for this product may not exist in your area.

All rights reserved. Except for use in any review, the reproduction or utilization of this work in whole or in part in any form by any electronic, mechanical or other means, now known or hereinafter invented, including xerography, photocopying and recording, or in any information storage or retrieval system, is forbidden without the written permission of the publisher, Harlequin Enterprises Limited, 225 Duncan Mill Road, Don Mills, Ontario M3B 3K9, Canada.

This is a work of fiction. Names, characters, places and incidents are either the product of the author's imagination or are used fictitiously, and any resemblance to actual persons, living or dead, business establishments, events or locales is entirely coincidental.

This edition published by arrangement with Harlequin Books S.A.

For questions and comments about the quality of this book, please contact us at CustomerService@Harlequin.com.

® and TM are trademarks of Harlequin Enterprises Limited or its corporate affiliates. Trademarks indicated with ® are registered in the United States Patent and Trademark Office, the Canadian Intellectual Property Office and in other countries.

HARLEQUIN®

www.Harlequin.com

Printed in U.S.A.

At Her Boss's Pleasure

CHAPTER ONE

FRIDAY. END OF JULY. Six-thirty in the evening...

And where, Kate thought, *am I?* Still in the office. She was the last man standing. Or sitting, in actual fact. At her desk, with the computer flickering in front of her and profit and loss columns demanding attention. Not *immediate* attention—nothing that couldn't wait until the following Monday morning—but...

She sighed and sat back, stretching out the knots in her shoulders, and for a few minutes allowed herself to get lost in thought.

She was twenty-seven years old and she knew where she should be right now—and it wasn't in the office. Even if it was a very nice office, in a more-than-very-nice building, in the prestigious heart of London.

In fact she should be anywhere but here.

She should be out enjoying herself, lazing around in Hyde Park with friends, drinking wine and luxuriating in the long, hot summer. Or having a barbecue in a back garden somewhere. Or maybe just sitting inside, with some music on in the background and a significant other discussing his day and asking about hers.

She blinked and the vision of possibilities vanished. Since moving to London four years ago she could count on the fingers of one hand the number of close friends she had managed to make, and since qualifying as an accountant and joining AP Logistics a year and a half ago she had made none.

Acquaintances, yes…but friends? No. She just wasn't the sort of outgoing, chirpy, confidence-sharing, giggling sort of girl who made friends easily and was always part of a group. She knew that and she rarely thought about it all—except… well…it was Friday, and outside the baking sun was fading into pleasant balmy warmth, and in the rest of the world people her age were all out there enjoying themselves. In Hyde Park. Or in those back gardens where barbecues were happening…

She glanced through her office door and an array of empty desks stared back at her accusingly, mockingly, pointing out her shortcomings.

She hurriedly made a mental list of all the wonderful upsides to her life.

Great job at one of the most prestigious companies in the country. Her own office, which was a remarkable achievement considering her age. Her own small one-bedroom flat in a nice enough area in West London. How many girls her age actually *owned* their own place? In London? Yes, there was a mortgage, but still…

She had done well.

So she might not be able to escape her past. But she could bury it so deeply that it could no longer affect her.

Except…

She *was* here, at work, on her own, on a Friday evening, on the twenty-sixth of July…

So what did *that* say?

She hunched back over the screen and decided to give herself another half an hour before she would leave the office and head back to her empty flat.

Thankfully she became so engrossed in the numbers staring back at her that she was barely aware of the distant ping of the lift and the sound of footsteps approaching the huge open-plan room where the secretaries and trainee accountants sat, and then moving on, heading towards her office.

She was squinting at the screen and totally un-aware of the tall, dark figure looming by the door until he spoke, and then she jumped and for a few unguarded seconds was not the cool, collected woman she usually was.

Alessandro Preda always seemed to have that effect on her.

There was something about the man…and it was more—much more—than the fact that he owned the company...this great big company that had dozens of satellite companies under its umbrella.

There was something about *him*... He was just so much larger than life, and *not* in a comforting, cuddly-bear kind of way.

'Sir... Mr Preda... How can I help you?' Kate leapt to her feet, smoothing down her neat grey skirt with one hand, tidying the bun at the nape of her neck with the other—not that it needed tidying.

Alessandro, who had been leaning indolently against the doorframe, sauntered into her office, which was the only area lit on this floor of his company.

'You can start by sitting back down, Kate. When I achieve royal status you can spring to your feet as I enter the room. Until then there's really no need.'

Kate plastered a polite smile on her lips and sat down. Alessandro Preda might be drop-dead gorgeous—all lean and bronzed and oozing sexy danger—but there was nothing about him *she* found in the least bit appealing.

Too many people were in awe of his brilliance. Too many women swooned at his feet like pathetic, helpless damsels in distress. And he was just too arrogant for his own good. He was the man who had it all, and he was very much aware of that fact.

But, since he literally owned the ground she walked on, she had no choice but to smile, smile, smile and hope he didn't see beneath the smile.

'And there's no need to call me *sir* every time you address me. Haven't I told you that before?'

Dark-as-night eyes swung in her direction and lazily inspected the cool, pale face that had not cracked a genuine smile in all the time she had been working at his company. At least not in *his* presence.

'Yes, you have…er…'

'Alessandro…the name is *Alessandro*. It's a family firm—I like to keep it casual with my employees…'

He swung round to perch on the edge of her desk and Kate automatically inched back in her chair.

Hardly a family firm, she thought sarcastically. *Unless your family runs into thousands and happens to be scattered to the four corners of the globe. Big family.*

'What can I do for you, Alessandro?'

'Actually, I came to leave some papers for Cape. Where is he? And why are *you* the only one alive and kicking here? Where are the rest of the accounts team?'

'It's after six-thirty…er…Alessandro… They all left a while ago…'

Alessandro consulted his watch and frowned. 'You're right. Not that it's stretching the outer limits of the imagination to think that at least a few members of my highly paid staff might be here. Working.' He looked at her, eyes narrowed. 'So what are *you* still doing here?'

'I had a few reports I wanted to get through before I left. It's a productive time of day…when everyone else has left for the evening…'

Alessandro looked at her consideringly, head tilted to one side.

What *was* it about this woman? He had had some dealings with her over the past few months. She was a hard worker, diligent, had been fast-tracked by George Cape. He certainly had not been able to fault the quickness of her mind. Indeed, she seemed to have a knack for cutting through the crap and finding the source of problems—which wasn't that easy in the fiddly arena of finance.

Everything about her was professional, but there was something *missing*.

The cool green eyes were guarded, the full mouth always tight and polite, the hair never out of place.

His eyes roved lower, taking in a body that was well sheathed behind a prim white long-sleeved shirt, neatly cuffed at the wrists and buttoned to the neck.

Outside, the temperatures had been soaring for the past three weeks—and yet you would never guess, looking at her, that it was summer beyond the office walls. He would bet his fortune that she would be wearing tights.

He, personally, thrived on a rich diet of sexy women who flaunted their assets, so Ms Kate Watson's severe veneer never failed to arouse his curiosity.

The last time he had worked with her—for several days, on a tricky tax issue with which she had seemed more adept at dealing than her boss, George Cape, whose head had recently been in the clouds—he had tried to find out a bit more about her. Had asked her a few questions about what she did outside work…her hobbies, her interests. Polite chit-chat as they had taken time out over the food that had been delivered to his office suite.

Most women responded to any interest he showed in them by opening up. They couldn't wait to tell him all about themselves. They preened and blossomed when he looked at them, when he listened to what they had to say, even though, in fairness, his attention wasn't always exclusively on what they were talking about.

Kate Watson? Not a bit of it. She had stared at him with those cool green eyes and had managed to divert the conversation without giving anything of herself away.

'You're here every evening at this hour?'

Still perched on her desk, invading her space, Alessandro picked up a glass paperweight in the shape of a goldfish and twirled it thoughtfully between his fingers.

'No, of course not.' *But far too often, all things considered.*

'No? Just today? Even though it's the hottest day of the year?'

'I'm not a big fan of hot weather.' She lowered her eyes, suddenly a little angry at some kind of unspoken, amused criticism behind his words. 'I find it makes me sluggish.'

'It would,' Alessandro pointed out, dumping the goldfish back on the desk where he had found it, 'if you wear long-sleeved shirts and starched skirts.'

'If you'd like to leave the papers with me, I'll make sure I give them to George when he's back.'

'Back from where?'

'He's on holiday at the moment. Canada. He's not due back for another two weeks.'

'*Two weeks!*'

'It's not that long. Most people book two-week holidays during summer…'

'Have you?'

'Well, no…but…'

'Not sure this can wait until Cape decides to grace us with his presence.'

He stood up and slapped a sheaf of papers on her desk, then placed his hands, palms down, squarely on either side of the papers and leaned into her.

'I asked Watson Russell if he knew anything about the anomalies in the supply chain to the leisure centres I'm setting up along the coastline and he told me that it's been Cape's baby from the start. True or false?'

'I believe he is in charge of those accounts.'

'You *believe*?'

Kate took a deep breath and did her utmost not to be intimidated by the man crowding her—but it was next to impossible. Tall, raven-haired, muscular and leaning into her, he didn't cause anything but a rapidly beating heart, a dry mouth and perspiring palms which she surreptitiously wiped on her skirt.

'He's in charge of those accounts. Exclusively. Perhaps you could explain what it is you'd like to find out?'

Alessandro pushed himself away from the desk and prowled through the office, noting in passing how little there was of her personality in it. No cutesy photographs in frames on the desk, no pot plants, no gimmicky pen-holder…not even a desk calendar with uplifting seascapes...or works of art...or adorable puppies...or semi-clad firemen...

He said nothing for a few seconds, then spun to face her, hands thrust deep into his trouser pockets.

'Quite by chance a batch of files was delivered to me—probably because "Private and Confidential" was stamped so boldly on the envelope that the post boy must have automatically headed up to the directors' floor. I scanned them and there appeared to be...how shall I say this?...certain discrepancies that need checking out.'

He couldn't keep his eye on every single small detail within his vast empire. He paid people very generously indeed to do that, and with the fat pay packet came a great deal of trust.

He trusted his people not to try and screw him over.

'There are a couple of small companies whose names I can't say I recognize. I may have a lot of companies, but generally speaking I do know what they're called...'

Kate paled as the significance of what he was saying began to sink in.

'You catch on quickly,' Alessandro said approvingly. 'I had actually come down here to confront Cape with these files, but in his absence it might be a better idea for *you* to have a look at them and collate whatever evidence is necessary.'

'Evidence? Necessary for what?' she asked faintly, and flushed when he raised his eyebrows in question, as if incredulous that the point of what he had said might have passed her by. 'George Cape is nearly at retirement age…he's a family man…he has a wife, kids, grandchildren…'

'Call me crazy,' Alessandro said, with such silky assurance that she wanted to throw the goldfish paperweight at his handsome head, 'but when someone I employ decides to take advantage of my generosity I tend to feel a little aggrieved. Of course I could be completely off target here. There might very well be a simple explanation for what I've seen…'

'But if there isn't…?' She was unwillingly mesmerized by the graceful way he moved around her small office, his jacket bunching where his hand was shoved in his trouser pocket.

'Well, the wheels of justice have to do *something* to keep busy…' He shrugged. 'So, here's how this is going to play out: I am officially going to hand the files over to you and you are to examine them minutely, from cover to cover. I am assuming you know Cape's password for his computer?'

'I'm afraid I don't.'

'In which case get one of the computer whizz-kids to sort that out. You're going to go through every single document that has been exchanged on this particular project and get back to me out of work hours.'

'Out of work hours? What are you talking about?'

'I think Cape's been embezzling,' Alessandro informed her bluntly. 'We could keep going round the houses, but that's the long and short of it. I had no idea that he was in sole charge of this project. Had he not been I might have been inclined to widen the net of suspicion, but it fundamentally comes down to just one man.'

He paused to stand in front of her desk and she reluctantly looked up—and up, and up—into his dark, lean face.

'From what I've seen there's not a great deal of money involved, which might be why no alarm bells went off, but not a great deal over a long period of time could potentially amount to a *very* great deal, and if there are dummy companies involved...'

'I hate the thought of checking into what George has been doing,' Kate said truthfully. 'He's such a lovely guy, and he's been good to me since I began working here. If it weren't for him I probably wouldn't have been promoted as quickly as I have been...'

'Blow his trumpet too vigorously and I might start thinking that you are in on whatever the hell's been going on.'

'I'm not,' she said coldly, her voice freezing over. Her green eyes held his. 'I would never cheat anyone of anything. That's not the sort of person I am.'

Alessandro's ears pricked up. He had dropped down to the third floor to deposit these papers with George Cape before heading out. He had no date—and no regret there either. His last blonde bombshell had gone the way of all good things, and he was back to the drawing board and more than happy to have a break from the fairer sex.

Kate Watson—*Ms* Kate Watson—was everything he avoided when it came to women. She was cold, distant, intense, unsmiling and prickly. She never let him forget that she was there to do a damn good job and nothing else.

But that single sentence…*That's not the sort of person I am*…had made him wonder.

What sort of person *was* she?

'You were asking me about my out-of-hours suggestion…' Alessandro moved the topic swiftly along, at the same time relegating her stray remark to a box from which it would be removed at a later date.

He had nothing to do on a Friday night. A rare situation for him. He dragged the single spare chair in the room across to her desk and sat down, angling it so that he could extend his long legs to the side, crossing them at the ankles.

Kate watched with something approaching horror. 'I was about to leave… Perhaps we could continue this conversation on Monday morning? I'm usually in first thing. By seven-thirty most days.'

'Laudable. It's heart-warming to know that there's at least one person in my finance department who doesn't clock-watch.'

'I'm sure you must have plans for the evening, sir…Alessandro. If I take the paperwork home I can have a look at it over the weekend and get back to you with my findings on Monday morning. How does that sound?'

'The reason I suggested that we discuss this situation out of hours is because I would rather not have it turned into a matter for speculation. Naturally you would be paid generously for your overtime.'

'It's not about being paid for overtime,' Kate said stiffly. She kept her eyes firmly pinned to his face, but she was all too aware of the lazy length of his body, the flex of muscles under the white shirt, the tanned column of his throat and the strength of his forearms where he had shoved the sleeves of his shirt to the elbows.

He had always made her jumpy, in a way other men never had. There was a raw, primal, barely contained aggression about him that threatened her composure, and it had done so from the very first time she had set eyes on him as a new recruit to the company.

It was dangerous. It was the sort of *dangerous* she could do without. She didn't like the way her body seemed to respond to him of its own accord. It frightened her.

Her upbringing had taught her many things, and the biggest thing it had taught her was the need for control. Control over her emotions, control over her finances, control over the destination of her life. She had grown up with a role model of a mother who had lacked all control.

Shirley Watson had adopted the frivolous name *Lilac* at the age of eighteen, and had spent her life living up to it—moving from pole dancer to cocktail-bar waitress to barmaid back to cocktail-bar waitress, flirting with men's magazine pin-ups along the way.

A stunningly beautiful, pocket-sized blonde, she had only ever learned how to exploit the natural assets with which she had been born. Kate only knew sketchy details of her mother's past, but she did know that Lilac had grown up as a foster-home kid. She had never known stability, and instead of trying to create some of her own had relied on being a dumb blonde, always believing that love lay just round the corner, that the men who slept with her really loved her.

Kate's father had vanished from the scene

shortly after she was born, leaving Lilac heartbroken at the age of just twenty-one. From him, she had moved on to a string of men—two of whom she had married and subsequently divorced in record time. In between the marriages she had devoted her life to pointlessly trying to attract men, always confusing their enthusiasm for her body for love, always distraught when they tired of her and pushed on.

She was a smart woman, but she had learned to conceal her brains because a brainy woman, she had once confided in her daughter, never got the guy.

Kate loved her mother, but she had always been painfully aware of her shortcomings and had determined from an early age that she would not live a life blighted by the same mistakes her mother had made.

It helped that she was dark-haired. And tall. She lacked her mother's obvious sex appeal and for that she was thankful. Her assets she kept firmly under wraps, and when it came to men…well…

Any man who liked her for her body was off the cards. No way was she ever going to fall into the same helpless trap her mother had. She relied on her brains, and goodness knew it had been tough going, ploughing through her school years, moving from place to place, never quite know-

ing what would confront her on her return home
from school.

Her mother, by a stroke of good fortune, had
been given sufficient money by her second husband in their subsequent divorce to enable her to
buy somewhere small in Cornwall. She—Kate—
would not be relying on any such stroke of fortune. She would provide for herself by hook or by
crook and be independent.

And when and if she ever fell in love it would
be with a guy who appreciated her intelligence,
who was not the kind of man with commitment
issues, who didn't abandon women after he had
had his fill of them, who didn't go out with women
because of the way they looked.

So far this paragon of virtue hadn't appeared
on the scene, but that didn't mean that she would
ever be distracted in the meantime by the sort of
guy she privately despised.

So why, she wondered, did her stupid body
begin a slow burn whenever Alessandro Preda
was within her radius?

And now here he was, making noises about
them working alongside one another *outside normal working hours*.

'Then what is it about?' Alessandro demanded,
bringing her back to the reality of him sitting
across from her with a bump. 'Hectic social life?
Can't spare a week to sort this matter out?' He

glanced around him before settling his dark eyes on her cool, pale face. 'Despite the extremely pleasant office you have here at the tender age of what…? Twenty-something…?'

'I've been promoted on merit.'

'And part of that promotion involves going beyond the call of duty now and again. Consider this one of those instances.'

Kate lowered her eyes, keeping her cool.

'You said you were heading off now…?'

'Yes.'

'In that case…' Alessandro stood up and sauntered towards the door, where he proceeded to lean against it, staring at her '…I'll walk you down. In fact, I'll go one better. I'll give you a lift to your house. Where do you live?'

Kate licked her lips nervously and ventured a polite smile as she stood up as well, and began tidying a desk that wasn't in need of tidying.

'How long have you been here?'

His voice had her head snapping up and she looked at him in bewilderment.

'How long have I been where? In your company? Working in London?'

'Let's start with in this office.'

Kate looked around her at her neat space, in which she felt so safely cocooned. These four walls were tangible proof of how far she'd come and how quickly—tangible proof of the solid income that marked her steps along that road called *financial security*.

Her mother had asked if she could visit her place of work when next she was in London but Kate had tactfully, and a little shamefully, killed the suggestion before it could take shape.

Lilac Watson, not yet fifty, and these days thankfully a little less obvious in displaying what she had to offer physically, would still never have blended into these muted, expensive surroundings.

This was Kate's life, built with her own blood, sweat and tears, and her mother had her own life. In Cornwall. Far away. Separate.

'What about it?' She shoved her work laptop into a leather briefcase and reached for the grey jacket she had slung over the back of her chair.

Grey jacket, grey calf-length skirt, flat, sensible patent pumps and, yes, definitely tights. Not stockings. *Tights.* Possibly of the support variety. Who knew? It was impossible to tell what sort of figure she had under the prim ensemble. Not fat, not thin, tall… The shirt managed to hide everything up top and the skirt did a similar job with everything down below.

And why the hell was he looking anyway?

'How long have you been here? *In* it?'

Kate paused and frowned. 'A little over six months. To start with I was moved in here because I was working late on a couple of very big clients and George thought that the quiet would help concentration. Not that it's a mad house outside. It isn't. And then, when I was promoted, I was offered it. I snapped it up.'

She reached for her briefcase, slung her black bag over her shoulder and straightened her skirt.

'Thanks very much for your offer of a ride home, but there are one or two things I need to collect on the way so I shall take the Tube.'

'What things?'

'Things… Food items. I need to stop off at the corner shop.'

Alessandro heard irritation behind her calmly spoken words. This was something he wasn't used to, and he was as bemused by his own reaction to it as he had been by his earlier curiosity as to what lay underneath the prissy work clothes.

'Not a problem.' He waved aside her objection. 'I've sent my driver home and I have my own car. Far more convenient if you load whatever you need to buy into my car rather than having to walk with it back to your house.'

'I'm accustomed to walking home with my groceries.'

Alessandro looked at her narrowly. He wouldn't have taken her for being skittish, but there was something skittish about her now. And why turn down a ride home? With him?

'It would be useful for us to decide how to

approach this delicate problem with George Cape and whatever money he's been siphoning off.'

'*If* he's been siphoning off any. And I was under the impression that you had already decided what you would do if you found out that he had taken money from you…throw him in prison and chuck away the keys.'

'Let's hope I've got it wrong, in that case, and he'll be spared the prison sentence.' He stepped aside, leaving her just sufficient room to brush past him through the door, switching off the lights in her wake. 'You've been in this office for six months and this is the first time it's struck me that there's nothing personal in here at all. *Nothing.*' Kate flushed. 'It's an office,' she said briskly, stepping in front of him, briefcase in one hand, bag over her shoulder, head held high and deliberately averted from him. 'Not a boudoir.'

'Boudoir…nice word. Is that where you stash all your personal mementoes? In your boudoir?'

Kate heard the amusement in his voice and turned to him angrily. *Get a grip*, she told herself sternly. *Don't let the man rattle you.* Green flashing eyes clashed with his oh-so-dark ones and she felt herself sinking into his gaze, had to yank herself firmly back to reality.

Alessandro Preda had a reputation with women. Even if the gossip hadn't reached her ears, one glance at any news rag would have informed her of that reputation.

He used women. He was always being snapped with models draped on his arm, gazing up at him adoringly. Lots of models. A different model for every month of the year. He could have started his own agency with the number of them he ran through. She wondered whether some of those models had been like her mother—sad creatures, blessed with spectacular looks but not enough common sense to know how to use what they had been given. Hanging on. Hoping for more than would ever be on the agenda.

'Shall I email you my findings?' Underneath the scrupulous politeness her voice could have frozen fire. She pressed the button to summon the lift and stared at him, as rigid as a plank of wood.

Alessandro had never seen anyone so uptight in his entire life.

This went way beyond self-control—way beyond a certain amount of composure.

What was her story? And didn't she know that all those 'No Trespassing' signs she'd erected around herself were enticing beacons to a man like him?

He was thirty-four years old, and he wasn't sure whether to be proud or simply accepting of the fact that he had never had to try very hard for a woman. They offered themselves to him.

But *Ms* Kate Watson had issues with him. He didn't know what they were, but he did know that they constituted a challenge—and since when had he ever been a man to turn down a challenge?

If he had, he certainly wouldn't have ended up in the exalted position of power that he had.

He suppressed the onslaught of thoughts that always managed to put him in a foul mood.

'I don't think so.' He stepped back as the lift doors slid open, allowing her to edge past him, making sure she kept her distance as much as she could, doing her utmost to be casual about it. 'Emails can be intercepted.'

'Aren't you being a bit cloak and dagger about all of this?'

Kate addressed the long metal case in the lift containing the various buttons, but she was acutely aware of him right next to her, of the warmth of his body wafting through the air and settling around her like a dangerous cloak that she wanted to shake off. She couldn't remember him having this sort of effect on her before, but then they had usually been in a room with other people around—not heading down in a lift, just the two of them.

She was alive to his presence in a way that made her whole body feel uncomfortable.

Alessandro stared at that pale averted profile. She was a beautiful woman, he realized with sudden surprise. It was something that wasn't immediately apparent, because she was at such pains to play down her looks, but studying her now he saw her features were perfect. Her nose was small and straight, her lips oddly full and sexy, her cheekbones high and sharp. Maybe the severity of her hairstyle accentuated all of that.

He wondered how long her hair was. Impossible to tell.

She swung round sharply and he straightened, flushing guiltily at being caught red-handed staring at her. *Not* very cool.

'I doubt George is going to do a runner if he gets wind that you're on to him. And that's *if* he's guilty of anything at all!'

'Why are you so keen to protect him?'

'I'm not keen to protect him. Just being fair. Innocent until proved guilty, and all that.'

The lift doors opened with a purr and she stepped out into the vast marbled foyer that still impressed her after nearly two years.

She wasn't protecting George Cape. Or was she? When she thought of George, a little guy staring down the barrel of a gun and not even realizing it, she thought of her own vulnerable mother, who had lived most of *her* life staring down the barrel of a gun and not realizing it, and when she thought about her mother she felt her heart constrict.

Which, of course, was *not* going to do. Least of all with a man like Alessandro Preda. And naturally she could see his point of view.

'Commendable,' Alessandro murmured. 'So we begin on Monday. The hunt to find out whether Cape is guilty of fraud or stupidity. Either way, he will doubtless end up being sacked. Now, where do you live...? My car's in the underground car park.'

CHAPTER TWO

IT HAD TAKEN a lot for Kate not to get in touch with George Cape over the weekend. *Was* he guilty of fraud? It was hard to believe. He was a true gentleman, courteous and kind, and he had taken her under his wing when she had started working for him. That said, he had not been his usual self over the past three months. Was there an explanation there somewhere?

She had looked through the files. Thankfully, no dummy companies had been set up—which she hoped ruled out fraud on a systematic large-scale basis. But the odd entries were definitely there, and...

She sighed and looked at her watch. She had managed to put off Alessandro the previous Friday evening, but he would be expecting her in his office now. At nearly seven p.m., the offices were again practically empty—aside from a few hard-core, nose-to-the-grindstone employees who barely glanced in her direction as she briskly walked out of the office with her files towards the bank of lifts.

It had been a while since she had been in Alessandro's office. Not since that tax problem that had needed sorting out. George and the head of finance had been there too, but there had been a brief period when it had just been her, doing the grunt work with the numbers, and Alessandro, who had been covering other aspects of the problem, and he had ordered in food for both of them.

It had been one of the few occasions when they had been alone together and she could still vividly recall the way she had burned when she had glanced up at one point and their eyes had met.

He had very dark eyes, fringed with thick, dark lashes, and that day he had had the sort of brooding, thoughtful expression that sent shivers racing up and down her spine. Having him look at her had felt like a very physical experience and she hadn't liked it.

And now that she was stepping into the lion's den again she was determined to bring her wayward reactions to heel.

Unfortunately her rapidly beating heart was already letting the side down, and by the time she heard that deep, masculine drawl telling her to enter her palms were sweaty and her nerves were all over the place.

He was sprawled in his leather chair, hands folded loosely on his stomach.

'Slight change of plan.'

They were his opening words and Kate stopped abruptly in her tracks. 'I could always leave the files and we can discuss them another time.' Disappointment warred with relief. 'If you're busy.' Her eyes flickered away from their compulsive visual tour of his body.

'We will discuss this over something to eat.'

That had her snapping to attention, and she looked at him with alarm. 'There's no need.' She had already recalled the last time they had shared a meal in this setting, and a repeat performance was something she could do without. 'I haven't managed to speak to the computer department about getting hold of George's password, but I don't think we will need to do that.' She took a few steps forward and thrust the files onto his desk. 'There are no dummy companies. I've checked that out thoroughly. And—'

'Over dinner.'

He slung his long body out of the chair and grabbed the jacket that had been tossed on the leather sofa by the wall. He didn't bother to put it on, preferring to hook it over his shoulder with his finger, and then he continued.

'I've asked you to work after hours. It's only

fair that I take you out to dinner. I mean, we do both have to eat...'

'I hadn't thought... This really won't take very long...'

Alessandro had paused to stand in front of her, his lean, muscular body radiating a power that sapped her energy and threw her into a state of confusion. She resented both things. She was the consummate professional—a woman whose composed, efficient veneer was never dented. She had devoted her whole life to controlling the sort of feminine weakness that had reduced her mother to a victim over the years.

To combat the treacherous ache in her body she tightened her jacket around her, buttoning it and standing straighter—ramrod straight.

'This is a man's future we're talking about,' Alessandro's keen eyes had noted all her little defence mechanisms: the way her lips had pursed, the tension in her shoulders, the buttoning of the jacket. 'You wouldn't want to write it off in a five-minute summary just because you happen to have a hot date for the evening, would you?'

'I don't have a hot date.'

The words left her mouth before she could drag them back, and it was no big deal but she still felt suddenly vulnerable and exposed. Her cheeks were burning as curious eyes lingered on her face.

'I...I prefer to stay in on week nights,' she

gamely went on, even though she knew she should just shut up, because now he was staring at her with even more curiosity. 'I often take work home with me. There's a lot to get through and I know how easy it is for…for…things to pile up…'

'You work late every evening, Kate. I don't imagine anyone would expect you to take work home with you as well.' He moved towards the door and opened it, standing back to allow her through. 'Which is all the more reason for me to take you out for dinner, so that we can discuss this in less formal surroundings. I wouldn't want you to see me as an unscrupulous boss who denies his employees a private life.'

Rattled, Kate walked briskly towards the lift. She turned to look at him. 'But aren't you?'

It was a daring question. One she shouldn't have asked. He represented everything she didn't like. In the normal course of events their paths would scarcely overlap. He rarely ventured down into the bowels of his offices, where the little people kept the wheels of his machinery well oiled and turning. But she didn't like what he did to her, what he did to her prized self-control, and some wicked little devil inside her had pushed her to be more daring than she normally would have been.

'Aren't I what?' He wondered how he had not noticed before the way her green eyes were the colour of polished glass.

Those polished-glass eyes slid sideways now.

'Unscrupulous.' Kate said eventually, although she still wasn't looking at him as the lift carried them downstairs in what felt like a step out of routine that she didn't want to take. Her heart was beating frantically inside her and she was thankful for the reliable armour of her neat starched suit. It gave her a confidence that was suddenly missing.

As they exited the building it was at least easier to talk to him when she was walking next to him and not staring directly at his face.

'What I'm saying is I thought that in order to make it to the top you would *have* to be unscrupulous. No one ever gets to play in the Champions League unless they're willing to…well…'

'Crush everyone and everything in their path?' He clasped her arm and turned her to face him.

'I didn't say that.'

'That's not my style. There's no need. And if this has to do with any decision I make about Cape, then you're way off target. If Cape's been defrauding my company then he'll take the consequences. It's an unfortunate truth that people must live and die by the decisions they make.'

'That seems a little harsh.'

'Does it?' His eyes darkened but he released her arm, even though he didn't immediately carry on walking. The crowds parted around them, shooting them curious looks.

Here, outside, it was very warm, and her suit of armour was beginning to feel more than a bit uncomfortable. Her skin prickled and she licked her lips nervously.

'Not that it's any of my business,' she was quick to add. 'Where are we going to eat?'

'Is that your way of telling me that you'd like to bring this conversation to an end?'

'I shouldn't have said…what I said.'

'You're free to speak your mind.'

They began walking to a gastropub that was tucked down one of the tiny side streets close to his offices in the heart of the city.

'Because it's really just a family firm…?' There was a smile in her voice as she tried to lighten the atmosphere.

'You've got it. One big, happy family—just so long as all my family members behave themselves. When one of them steps out of line, then I'm afraid I have to rule with a firm hand.'

'It's a very *big* family.'

'Which started small. And I suppose that's why it's important for me to take control when a situation such as the one we have now develops. I didn't create this baby for anyone to get it into their heads that they could climb on my bandwagon and begin looting. Here we are.'

He pushed open the door into a space that was so dark it took Kate a couple of seconds for her eyes to adjust. Dark and refreshingly cool, and quaintly higgledy-piggledy.

'This is not the sort of place I thought you would have liked,' she blurted out impulsively, and Alessandro smiled.

'I'm old friends with the man who owns it, and as a matter of fact coming here is something of an antidote to my frenetic pace of life. Why don't you take your jacket off?'

'I'm fine.'

Alessandro raised his eyebrows with mild disbelief. 'I expect you'd like to get down to work immediately…bypass all the pleasantries…?'

'I have all the files in my briefcase.'

'I hate to curb your enthusiasm, but I could do with relaxing for five minutes before I begin to hear about what George Cape's been up to. You might think I'm hard-line, but Cape's been with my company for a quite a number of years. It's regrettable that he could not have just approached me had he wanted a loan.'

She was spared the temptation of telling him that perhaps he needed to work on the whole *family atmosphere* approach by the arrival of the owner of the restaurant, who made a great fuss of Alessandro. They lapsed into rapid Italian and she covertly watched Alessandro, relaxed, gesticulating, grinning, showing her a natural warmth that was usually concealed under the forbidding exterior.

This would be the man who charmed women, she thought. The guy who could have any woman he wanted at the snap of a finger and made full use of the talent.

And, of course, none of those women were Plain Janes or, God forbid, downright *unappealing*.

Drawn into their conversation towards the end, she smiled politely and offered the owner her hand in a businesslike handshake which, as they moved towards a table nestled in its own alcove towards the back of the restaurant, Alessandro told her had successfully nipped his friend's salacious ideas in the bud.

'I have no idea what you're talking about.' Once seated, she pointedly extracted the file they would need to discuss and placed it on the table next to her.

Wine was brought to them. On the house.

'You must know the proprietor very well,' she murmured, 'if free wine is part of the deal when you come here.'

'He would throw in free food as well.' Alessandro sat back and looked at her with lazy consideration. 'But I always insist on paying for what I eat.'

'That's very thoughtful of you.'

He laughed aloud and shot her an appreciative look. 'You have a sense of humour! I never realized.'

Kate thought that that was borderline rude, but how could she object when she had been pretty outspoken in some of the things she had said to *him*?

'Relax,' he urged, gently removing the hand that she held over her wine glass and pouring her some wine. 'We might be here to work, but you're not in the office now.'

And that, she thought, was the problem—because when she was in the office, surrounded by computers and filing cabinets and desks, and the constant buzz of ringing phones, she could be a cool, controlled professional. Whereas here...

The place was popular. Nearly every table was occupied, and the bar area was crowded with men in suits and women in sharp summer outfits and high heels.

'Why do you work so much overtime?'

Kate frowned and played with her wine glass before taking a sip. *What sort of a question is that?* she wanted to ask. He owned the company. Surely he should be congratulating her on her dedication to her job instead of asking her why she worked so hard?

'I thought that was the way to get ahead,' she said neutrally. 'But I might be mistaken.'

Alessandro grinned, enjoying her understated dry sense of humour.

'I mean,' Kate continued, warming to her theme because somehow, somewhere in his remark, there had been just the faintest hint of criticism. 'You *did* express some disappointment that the entire floor was empty when you came to drop those files off for George…'

'Quite true.'

'So why are you criticizing me because I happen to do a bit of overtime now and again?'

'I got the impression that it was more the rule than the exception. And I'm not criticizing you.'

'It sounds as though you are.' She could feel those dark eyes boring into her and had to restrain herself from squirming.

He was her *boss*. Actually, he was the lord of all he surveyed, and it was in her interests to remain as polite and detached as possible. Never mind all that tosh about his hundred-thousand-strong *family* of employees…he could ruin her career with the snap of his fingers. As he would doubtless ruin George Cape's career.

She bristled with anger, stole a resentful glance at his lean, beautiful face, and wondered what it would feel like to have those sensuous lips on hers.

She didn't even know where that errant thought had come from, but it was so vivid that her whole body responded. Her breasts ached, and between her legs...she was horrified to realize that she was dampening.

'I'm ambitious,' she told him heatedly, 'and there's nothing wrong with that. I work hard because I hope that my hard work will pay off, that I'll be promoted... I wasn't born with a silver spoon in my mouth and I've had to fight for every single thing I've got.'

It was more than she should have said, although not a word of it was untrue. It just felt weird—*wrong*—to be confiding in him. And why was she anyway? She wasn't here for an interview and he hadn't demanded that she explain herself.

Usually so reticent, she had been propelled into speaking her mind. She licked her lips nervously, realized that she was sitting forward, fists clenched on the table, and deliberately made herself relax and smile.

'You're implying that your colleagues come from a more privileged background than you?'

'I'm not implying anything. I was just...stating a fact.'

Alessandro noted the pink in her cheeks. Up close and personal with her—which he had never been before—he sensed that her reactions were honest. She blushed when he wouldn't have expected her to, because the impression she gave was one of complete self-control. He could remember asking her questions about certain technicalities in the jobs she had worked on and she had been cool, calm and knowledgeable, barely displaying any kind of personality at all.

But then…

He glanced briefly around him. This wasn't a cold, clinical office, was it? The neat little folder she had pointedly stuck on the table next to her was the only evidence that this was a work meeting. And without the backup of an office he had a tantalizing glimpse of the person behind the beautiful but bland exterior.

Did he want to bring the conversation back to work? Not yet.

'Maybe you think that *I* do…?' he murmured in a lazy drawl.

'I haven't given that any thought at all,' Kate lied. 'I'm here to do a job, not to pry into other people's lives.'

'Your days must be very dull, in that case.'

'Why? Why do you say that?'

'Because it's commendable to work hard, and to do a good job, but doesn't everyone get a little titillation from office politics? The salacious gossip? The speculating…?'

'Not me.'

Her voice was firm but her nerves were all over the place. She picked up the menu and stared at it but she could still feel his eyes on her.

'I think I might have the fish.'

Alessandro didn't bother to glance at the menu. He responded by keeping his eyes firmly fixed on her face while he beckoned with a slight raising of his hand and was rewarded when someone sprang to attention and hustled over.

How did he *do* that? Was there some poor sap hovering in the corner somewhere, waiting until the Mighty One beckoned him across?

Of course there would be. Money talked, and Alessandro Preda had a lot of it. Vast amounts.

People changed when they were around money. Common sense flew through the window. Subservience, slavishness and an awestruck inability to just *act normally* set in.

So she might feel *something*—a little insignificant twinge of awareness about the man—but that was natural. He was drop-dead gorgeous, especially when she was receiving the full, undiluted blast of his forceful personality. But she wasn't and never would be one of those simpering airheads who turned to mush around him. And actually not just airheads. Lots of clever women— definitely two in the legal department—giggled at the mention of his name and projected crazy fantasies about him over lunch in the office restaurant. Several times Kate had had to stop her eyes from rolling skywards.

Her body might be a little rebellious, but thankfully she had her head firmly screwed on.

She politely waited as he ordered, said no to a top-up of wine, and then relented because at least it made her relax.

'So, about George...' She flicked open the file and felt the weight of his hand over hers.

'In good time.'

'Sorry. I thought you might have finished relaxing.' Her heart was thumping so hard that she wondered if she might be having a mild panic attack. Or, worse, turning into one of those simpering airheads. Or even worse than that, one of those clever women whose brains went missing in action the second he came too close.

'Only just beginning.'

He dealt her a slashing smile that did nothing to steady her disobedient body and she pursed her lips in response.

'Perhaps I should have taken more of an interest in your career before...considering you're one of my rising stars...'

'I didn't think you got involved in doing appraisals on anybody in your company,' Kate responded politely. *Boss/employee*, she reminded herself. The boss got to ask all the questions and the employee got to ask none whatsoever.

'True,' Alessandro conceded.

He didn't look at the waiter as he placed their

food in front of them and then did some annoying perfect positioning of their plates. All he wanted the man to do was disappear. Because he was pleasantly invigorated and didn't want to lose the moment. They were few and far between as it was.

'I like to think that's what my human resources people are all about. Although, in fairness, they probably work to rule like the rest of the occupants of your floor.'

'Everyone works overtime in the winter months. It's just that it's summer and it's baking hot outside—I guess they want to leave on time and enjoy the sunshine.'

'But not you?' Alessandro pointed out. 'Nothing urgent out of hours waiting for you?'

'I don't think what I do outside work is actually any of your business—and I apologize right now if you think I'm being rude when I say that.'

'No need for apologies. I just want to make sure. Do you feel the need to live in the office in order to get on?'

'I…'

She tried to imagine living a life in which that mythical other half was right now whipping up something in the kitchen for her, anxiously consulting his watch if she was running late. She would have to do something about that—turn the passing thought into reality. She didn't miss having a guy in her life now, but she would eventually. She wasn't meant to be an island, and if she wasn't careful she would wake up one day and find herself alone because she had sacrificed everything to her quest for security.

'Tell me what you're thinking.'

'Huh?'

'You're a million miles away,' Alessandro drawled drily. 'Simple question, really. I didn't think it would have required that much deep thought.'

'I…'

For a few seconds she nearly told him just how much deep thought that 'simple question' required. More than he could ever imagine because—like it or not—this man who saw his vast empire as a family affair was a man who came from money. How could he ever understand the drive inside her to fill all the gaps her upbringing had left?

'Sorry… No. Of course I know that there's no need for me to work long hours to get on—although, in fairness, I probably work fewer hours in winter than my colleagues.'

'Ah, yes. Because you're a creature of the night?'

And just like that Kate thought of her mother, of those jobs in dark bars earning money from tips, dancing and showing herself off in whatever nonsense she was told to put on. A creature of the night doing night-time jobs. *Nothing like her.*

'Don't you *ever* say that to me!' she blurted out before she could stop herself. She was shaking with anger and stuck her hands under the table on her lap so that he couldn't see that they were shaking.

'Say what?' Alessandro asked slowly, his sharp eyes narrowed on her flushed face. 'Did I say something wrong?' He frowned and saw her make a visible effort to gather herself. 'Tell me what the problem is.'

'There isn't a problem. I'm sorry. I overreacted.'

'Firstly, stop apologizing for everything you say that you think might offend me. I don't take offence easily. And secondly…there *is* a problem. You went as white as a sheet and now you're shaking like a leaf. What provoked that sudden bout of outrage?'

Curiosity dug deep. Underneath the calm surface, she was a hotbed of emotion and that intrigued him. He leaned forward, elbows on the table, crowding her.

'You're trying to think of a polite way of telling me that it's none of my business, aren't you?'

Kate shied away from his searching narrowed stare. She could feel the full force of his powerful personality like something raw and physical and it appalled and mesmerized her at the same time. This was evidence of the driving tenacity that had propelled him into the stratosphere of wealth and power and it went far, far beyond his formidable intelligence and his ambition.

She averted her face, her heart beating wildly. 'My mother worked in a cocktail bar,' she said flatly.

Why had she just come out with that? She never, ever went there with other people. Her past was a closed book to prying eyes.

'Amongst other things. I have no idea why I'm telling you this.' She looked at him accusingly from under lowered lashes. 'I don't usually confide in other people. I'm not usually a confiding kind of person. I know you think I'm strange, working long hours, but...'

'But you crave financial security?'

'*Crave* is a strong word.' She smiled tentatively. 'But maybe it's the right one.'

She felt a weird sense of release at unburdening herself. When she was growing up, those sensitive teenage years had been an agony of embarrassment. She had made sure never to get too close to anyone. She hadn't wanted them to find out that her mother worked as a cocktail waitress, brought men home who used her because of the way she looked, was a sad, desperate woman who knew only how to barter with her body to keep them going.

She'd loved her mother but she had been ashamed of her—and ashamed of being ashamed.

And now here was her boss, Alessandro Preda, whose lifestyle repulsed her, who represented everything she found distasteful in a man, and the sympathy on his face was like a key unlocking her secrets. Stupid. Really stupid. *And somehow dangerous...*

'My upbringing was...unsteady. Mum never seemed interested in holding down a normal office job. I can only remember her going out at night, leaving me with some friend or other when I was young, and then the minute I hit twelve I was on my own. I loved my mother...I *love* my mother...but I hated the way she earned a living. I hated thinking of her in stupid skimpy clothes, with men staring and trying to paw her. And she was always falling in love—always thinking that Mr Right was the next handsome guy who paid her some attention and told her she was beautiful.'

'So when I called you a creature of the night...'

'I'm sorry.' Mortified, Kate stared at her empty wine glass and watched as he poured her some more wine. She hadn't planned on drinking anything at all. Now she wondered how much she had inadvertently downed. Maybe the alcohol had loosened her tongue? She didn't *feel* in the least bit tipsy, but why else would she have suddenly turned into a blabbering mess?

'What did I tell you about apologizing?'

'I work for you...'

'Which doesn't turn you into one of my subjects. Like I said, I have yet to attain royal status,' Alessandro drawled. 'Where does your mother live now?'

'Cornwall.' Kate shot him a quick glance and looked away just as fast.

He was just so sinfully *good-looking*! It shouldn't do anything for her, because she was the last person on the planet to judge a guy by the way he looked, but her tummy was in knots and she had to force herself not to stare at that dark, brooding, *interested* face. She almost had the feeling that, given half a chance, he would be able to reach into her head and pull out her deepest, darkest thoughts.

'She…she married twice. Her second husband, Greg, gave her sufficient money in their divorce for her to buy somewhere small, and she wanted to be by the sea.'

'And your father?'

'I had no idea I would be subjected to a question-and-answer session…' But she had initiated this whole conversation, and there was a weary acceptance of that in her voice.

Alessandro had never had the slightest curiosity about the back stories of his women. He was curious now.

'My father left soon after I was born. He was my mother's first love and her only love—so she tells me.' She cleared her throat and searched for the brisk, businesslike voice that was so much part and parcel of her persona. Sadly it was nowhere to be found. Just when she really felt she needed it. 'I think she's been trying ever since to replace him.'

'And now?'

'And now what?'

'There's someone in her life?'

Kate smiled and Alessandro felt the breath catch in his throat—a sudden, sharp, shocking reaction that came from nowhere. The woman was *beautiful*. Did she deliberately downplay that? This was a Pandora's box. She worked for him, and they were here to discuss the future of an employee. Serious stuff. But for the life of him he didn't want to let the conversation go.

'I'm proud to announce that my mother has been a man-free zone for three years. I feel she might be cured of her addiction to looking for love in all the wrong places.'

'And what about you?' Alessandro murmured huskily. 'Are *you* a man-free zone at the moment?'

His thoughts veered wildly into uncharted territory. He pictured her with a man. He pictured her with *him*. The face she chose to show the world was not the sum total of the person she was. In fact, scratch the surface and the cool, marble exterior gave way to swirling, unpredictable currents.

He had a driving, crazy urge to *test those waters*.

He had his own reasons, he knew, for the choices he had made and continued to make. His own parents and their all-consuming love had left little room for a kid and no room at all for common sense. Theirs had been a world with room only for each other, and their ridiculous choices had seen their joint family fortunes whittled away into nothing thanks to rash decisions, stupid blunders, irrational money-making ventures.

Control? They had had none of that. *He* did. He controlled every aspect of his life, including his love life, but suddenly all those beautiful, vapid, utterly controllable women who had cluttered his life seemed like *safe, dreary options*.

Insane. He had never mixed business with pleasure. *Never.* This woman was off limits.

But she had kick-started his libido and he felt the thrust of a powerful erection pressing against the zipper of his trousers, bulging and uncomfortable.

Kate detected something in his voice that sent the thrill of a shiver racing through her and desperately tried to squelch it.

How the heck had this happened? How had the conversation swerved from George and his misdeeds to questions about her private life? What on earth had possessed her to start sharing her life story like an idiot?

'I've been very busy getting my career up and

going,' she said briskly. 'I haven't had time to cultivate relationships.'

'All work and no play...' Alessandro murmured. 'Personally, I've always found that a little bit of play makes the work go a helluva lot faster.'

'That approach doesn't work for me. It never has.' She winced at the tenor of her voice—cold, prim, defensive. 'And now I think we ought to get the bill. I...it's later than I expected... I don't think it would be fair on George if we shoved our discussion of his plight into a few minutes tacked on to the end of a meal. I realize you've written him off as a master criminal, but I feel he deserves better than that.'

She automatically felt for the bun at the back of her head. Still firmly in place. Unlike the rest of her.

Alessandro mentally waved aside the topic of hapless George and his unfortunate wrongdoings. Tomorrow was another day. He would deal with that later. *They* would deal with that later. Right now...

'What approach doesn't work for you?'

Kate pretended to misunderstand his question.

'Ah. You've decided to retreat behind your professional mask. Why?'

'Because we didn't come here to talk about *me*. We came to talk about George.'

'But we didn't,' Alessandro pointed out with

remorseless logic. 'We didn't end up talking about George, as it happens.'

'And that was a mistake.' She breathed a silent sigh of relief as the bill was brought to them, and then breathed an even bigger sigh of relief when the proprietor approached and began enthusiastically quizzing them on what they thought of their meal, his sharp black eyes dancing between the two of them.

So she hadn't answered his question. And he wasn't sure why he wanted to find out anyway. But he did. What was it they said about wanting what you couldn't get?

He watched as she rose, terminating all personal conversation.

'I shall get a taxi home,' she told him firmly.

He ignored her. 'I wouldn't dream of it.'

He ushered her out into a much cooler evening—suitable weather finally for her starchy suit and jacket. He made a call on his cell phone and his car, complete with driver, appeared from nowhere. It pulled over and he opened the passenger door for her. When she was inside, he leant down so that he was looking at her on eye level.

'You'll be happy to know that you'll be spared my company.'

He grinned, and she had one of those intuitive moments of knowing that he knew exactly what had been going through her head.

'I'll get.Jackson to drop you home and we can pick up where we left off at a later date.'

'What later date?' She worried at her lower lip. If she could stick a few definite meetings in her work diary then she would be able to get a handle on seeing him again. And over her dead body if it was going to be in another cosy little restaurant.

'I'll get back to you on that one.'

'But don't you want to get this mess sorted out as quickly as possible?'

'You can keep an eye on all the business accounts for suspicious activity, but if there's none then why not let George enjoy his last supper, so to speak?' He stood up, slapped the hood of the sleek, black Maserati, and remained watching as it disappeared from view.

He hadn't felt so invigorated for a long time.

And what, he wondered, was a guy to do about *that*?

CHAPTER THREE

FOR THE PAST few years Kate had seen her place of work as a refuge. There, she had felt in charge of her life, had worked hard at putting together all the building blocks that gave it definition and purpose.

Now she felt jumpy. On tenterhooks. Always on the lookout for Alessandro who, for the past couple of days, had often appeared to talk to her. About a client with a thorny tax problem, two overseas companies whose vast returns had generated questions about splitting them into smaller fragments, an acquisition that would mark a significant branching out from electronics, shipping and the leisure industry into publications…

'Cape would normally handle this, but seeing that he's on an extended holiday abroad, and seeing that that extended holiday is likely to become permanent, you'd better start getting acquainted with some of his responsibilities…'

This at five-thirty earlier today, when most of her colleagues had mentally switched off in preparation for leaving and had been all agog at the appearance of the big man.

She had kept as cool and collected as she could but her nerves had been all over the place. Surely the head of finance should be handling this situation? she had ventured, watching askance as he had perched on the side of her desk and then dragging her eyes away from his muscular thighs and the way the fine fabric of his trousers was stretched taut over them. But, no. Watson Russell was swamped by several huge ongoing deals— and besides, these matters would qualify as fairly small peanuts for him.

Afterwards, some of the girls had hovered, waiting for her to emerge from her office, and had proceeded to ply her with questions. None of the questions had had anything to do with work. They had wanted her opinion of him. As a hunk. Kate had made it a point never to engage in conversations like that, but she had been pinned to the wall and had found herself admitting that he was all right but not her type.

So how come he's been around so much...is something going on...?

Argh! She had become just the sort of giggly, girly type she had never been, and it had left her all hot and bothered.

And he *still* hadn't committed to a meeting so that he could look through what she had found out—which, as it turned out, was not very much at all. George *had* been dipping his hands in the till, but it hadn't been going on for very long and the amounts, in the big scheme of things, weren't that significant.

She would talk to Alessandro about that—try and find some compassion in him for the older man—but she didn't hold out much hope.

Now, at home far earlier than she normally would have been, on yet another hot summer evening, Kate looked at her work computer with jaundiced eyes.

It wasn't yet six and she couldn't face sitting in front of her computer and picking up where she had left off during the day.

Wandering through her very nice little ground-floor flat, she had plenty of time to think about the social life she lacked.

The back door was flung open and she could smell the neighbours barbecuing. Aside from the pleasant couple with two kids living next to her, she had no idea who her neighbours were.

At work, having almost given up on asking her, two of her colleagues had invited her to go to the pub with them and she had felt a little surge of panic because...

Because her whole life was devoted to work.

How had that happened? Okay, she knew *how*, and she knew *why*, she just didn't understand how it had all run away with her so that she had lost all her perspective.

Not only was her social life practically non-existent, but where was the guy she should be dating? Where was the exciting sex life she should be having?

She had had one boyfriend, three years previously, and he had fallen off the face of the earth because he had wanted more attention than she had been prepared to give. He hadn't understood that she had been taking professional exams and had had to study when she wasn't holding down the demanding job at the accountancy firm she had left as soon as she had qualified.

At the time she had been miffed—because how hard would it have been for him to just give her some breathing space? Surely it had been enough that they'd had fun on the weekends? But he had wanted more than just fun on the weekends.

So now here she was—alone. She wouldn't have wanted to be with Sam still. No, in retrospect, he hadn't been the man for her, even though he had ticked a lot of the right boxes. But shouldn't she have *moved on*? Be having a good time finding his replacement? Somewhere?

She lived in *London*, for heaven's sake!

Frustrated with the direction of her thoughts, she slammed shut the French doors at the back so that she couldn't be reminded of what she was missing by the smell of barbecue wafting into her house.

Then she had a shower.

Then, in a pair of tiny shorts and a cropped top, she prepared to wait out the annoying train of thoughts that were suddenly bothering her.

For which she blamed her wretched boss, who had somehow managed to get under her skin, to make her feel somehow *inadequate*…

And as soon as she started thinking about Alessandro she found that she couldn't stop.

He was just so *alive* and *vital* and brimming over with restless energy. Next to him, she felt like a pale, listless shadow, going through the motions of having a fulfilling life when she wasn't.

Absorbed in pointless speculation, she was only aware of the doorbell when it was depressed with such insistency that she was forced to dash and pull open the door or else risk her neighbours complaining about noise pollution.

Alessandro Preda was the last person she'd expected to see standing on her doorstep. In fact she blinked rapidly, trying to clear her vision and turn him into someone else. But, no, he was still there. Tall, dynamic, broad-shouldered, and way too exotically good-looking for London suburbia.

He didn't say a word. Just looked at her. He had obviously come straight from work because he was still in his work trousers—charcoal grey, super conventional, and yet on him somehow *not quite*. But there was no jacket, and he had shoved the sleeves of his shirt up to his elbows, revealing muscled forearms liberally sprinkled with dark hair.

She seemed to have forgotten how to speak.

'Are you going to ask me in?'

Alessandro eventually broke the silence. It took some effort. He had wanted to catch her by surprise, had been driven by sheer curiosity to see her somewhere—anywhere—that wasn't to do with the office.

But he hadn't expected *this*.

This wasn't the starchy woman who occupied her own office three floors down in his building. Removed from the files, the computers, the telephones and the uninspiring range of suits in various shades of grey, this was a different woman altogether.

This was the woman he had glimpsed at the restaurant.

She was in a pair of shorts and a small top, and her hair was long and tied back in a ponytail that swung down her back.

Where had that body come from? She was long and slender, her stomach flat, her breasts…

He broke out in a fine film of perspiration. It was the sort of reaction he never experienced, and his awareness of her, his *physical* awareness of her, was intense, immediate—a rush of blood invading his body in a tidal surge.

She wasn't wearing a bra.

'What are you doing here?'

It was a breathless, angry question. She could barely deal with him at the office—was at war with herself and her puzzling reaction to him. How dared he now take himself out of that environment, which didn't even feel *safe* any more, and superimpose himself here? On her doorstep? In her apartment?

Suddenly excruciatingly aware of just how much of her body was exposed, she hugged her arms around herself and remained rooted to the spot. She hadn't shut the door in his face, but she wasn't inviting him in either.

'I've been busy this week,' Alessandro imparted roughly, raking fingers through his dark hair and staring away to one side while he tried to do the unimaginable and compose himself. 'I had every intention of going through this business with you, but I haven't had time. Like you said, Cape deserves more than five minutes of my attention when I can grab a moment.'

'You managed to grab lots of moments when you were in my office—piling work on me before George has even been given a decent burial...'

'Hell, why do you have to be so dramatic? And are you going to ask me in? Or am I going to have to stand outside and have this conversation with you? The neighbours might begin to wonder what's going on.'

Kate spun round on her heels, agonisingly conscious of her small shorts. She realized in a flash how important her formal work attire was. All those bland, off-the-peg suits in drab colours had been her way of keeping the rest of the world at bay. Even at the restaurant with him, when she had dropped her mask and actually spoken her mind, that suit of hers had still been a reminder of their respective roles.

But shorts and a cropped top? Since when could anyone call *that* armour?

Alessandro watched her extremely pert bottom as she stalked away from him. His erection was so ramrod hard that it was painful—and more than likely visible.

He wanted to ask her whether she made it a habit to open the door to anybody who might ring the bell dressed in next to nothing, because this wasn't Cornwall. He shoved both hands into his trouser pockets in an attempt to do some damage limitation with the serious bulge of his arousal.

'I'm going to change,' she told him ungraciously as she stood aside and indicated that he could wait for her in the kitchen. 'I'm sorry, Alessandro. I realize that you're the boss, and you probably think that you can do whatever you please, but I really don't think it's on for you to just call by unannounced.'

Her arms were still folded as she swung to look at him. Her heart picked up pace as their eyes tangled and held. Her skin felt too tight for her body. His eyes on her made her nipples tingle, made her want to rub her legs together to ease the ache between them.

'Why?'

He was now sitting at the kitchen table. *Thank God.* What the hell was going on here? He'd had his fill of stunning women, and none had had such an instantaneous effect on his libido. Was it because of the dichotomy between the consummate professional and the rangy, leggy, sexy woman she was under the uniform she chose to wear? Maybe it had been too long since he had had sex… He was a man with a high sex drive, and using his hand to do the job was far from satisfactory, given the choice of a woman's mouth doing the job for him.

He thought of Kate's mouth there, her pink tongue delicately flicking over his arousal, and he sucked in a sharp breath.

'Yes…' He cleared his throat. 'Go and change if it would make you feel better to slip into your suit because I'm here and you find it impossible to be anything in my company aside from an employee.'

'What's *that* supposed to mean?' Kate enquired tightly.

Alessandro sighed and sat back. 'It doesn't mean anything, Kate.'

It means you should leave now and return decently clothed. Sackcloth might do the trick.

'And you're right. I had no business showing up here on your doorstep without calling you in advance.'

'How did you know where I lived anyway?'

'Jackson was kind enough to provide me with the information.'

'And *that's* another thing,' she retorted, bristling as she thought back to her colleagues at work and their reactions to Alessandro descending from Mount Olympus to grace them with his presence. 'People have been talking...'

She reddened, but now that it was out what choice did she have but to stand her ground and say what was on her mind? Besides, he was in *her* territory now. If she couldn't speak freely in her own house, then where could she? He might be the ruler of all he surveyed in his towering glass house in the City, but he wasn't out here.

She quailed. Did he have to look so...so *ruler-like* even when he wasn't in his domain? She wished he would just look a little more *normal*, a little less...*intimidating*. Or sexy. Take your pick.

She suddenly felt her youth, her lack of experience.

'Talking?' Alessandro tilted his head to one side and looked at her intently. 'Talking about what? And who are these "people" who have been talking?'

'I maybe shouldn't have brought this up...' she began, chickening out.

'But you did, and now that you have you might as well finish. And for God's sake don't launch into any full-blown apologies when you've said what you want to say.'

'You seldom come down to our floor. In fact, I can only think of one time when you actually came to see me in my office, and George was there as well. Suddenly you've been appearing out of the blue and people...well, people have been wondering what's going on. They think... I don't know what they think... But I don't want them to think it. Whatever it is.'

'So these people think something...you're not sure what...and you don't want them to think it...?'

'I'm a very private person. Always have been.'

Except for one night in a restaurant, when I spilled my guts about my background to you...

'I'm at a loss as to what I can do to resolve this issue...'

He spread his arms wide in a typical gesture

that was at once rueful and ridiculously phoney, because there was just a hint of a smile tugging at the corners of his mouth that made her feel like an idiot. His brows knitted in a frown which was also phoney.

'I guess you must think that Jackson thinks something too…although who knows for sure…?'

'It's all well and good for you to sit there sniggering, but I'm the one who has to live with other people's stupid speculations!'

'That's office life for you. Maybe you should climb out of your ivory tower and experience it. And don't worry about Jackson, by the way. Whatever he might think, or not think, he'll keep it to himself.'

Kate gritted her teeth together and remembered diplomacy. He was rich, and immune to the opinions of other people. Not that there would be many people willing to shoot their mouths off at him. The man was unbearably arrogant in his self-confidence. And he talked about *her* living in an ivory tower!

'Maybe I should,' she said, with a tight, forced smile.

'You look as though you've swallowed a lime.' Alessandro grinned. He hadn't noticed her freckles before, or the fact that her dark hair was more chestnut than brown, and golden at the ends.

'I'm going to change. If you want something

to drink there's an opened bottle of wine in the fridge, or you can make yourself tea or coffee. It's not a big kitchen. I'm sure you'll be able to find what you need.'

With that she swung round and headed to her bedroom, fuming at the way he had invaded her privacy, fuming at the way he saw fit to say exactly what happened to be on his mind, fuming at her evening, which she had had neatly planned and which would now be spent in a state of edge-of-the-seat nervous tension.

She got to her bedroom and gazed at her mutinous reflection in the mirror. Her colour was up. Her hair was not in the neat little bun he was accustomed to seeing. The ponytail was coming undone and wisps of long brown hair trailed around her face. Which was completely bare of make-up…

She peered at the freckles which had always made her look so young.

Freckles, dishevelled hair, a pair of shorts that she would never in a million years have worn had she known that he—or anyone else, for that matter—would be turning up on her doorstep, and a small stretch top with no bra. The top might be navy blue, but she had generous breasts and it was perfectly obvious that they were not constrained.

If she half squinted and stood back just a tiny bit…well, she might pass muster as one of those cocktail waitresses she scorned. Small clothes, busty, legs everywhere, hair everywhere...

In the rational part of her mind Kate knew that it was just her imagination playing tricks on her. She wasn't dressed any differently from any young woman hanging around in her own home on a balmy summer evening.

But this was her tender spot—the place where her imagination took flight. She was ultrasensitive to any suggestion that she and her mother had *anything* in common when it came to the way they saw themselves and their bodies. Her mother had always been a benchmark as to how she, Kate, would *never* conduct herself.

She closed her eyes, breathed deeply, and hurriedly removed the offending attire, replacing the shorts and cropped top with a pair of jeans and a very sensible baggy tee shirt which revealed nothing but a faded logo on the front. She neatened up the ponytail, but drew the line at turning it into a bun.

When she made it back to the kitchen it was to find Alessandro well ensconced at her kitchen table, a glass of wine next to him, long legs extended to one side, relaxing back with his hands folded behind his head.

'I like your place.' He watched as she hovered for a few seconds by the kitchen door, the very picture of the disgruntled and reluctant host.

'Cool, airy, light colours… And nice that it's not in a big, impersonal block of flats as well. I take it there's just the one other flat above you…?'

'You've been poking around…' she said, eyes narrowed.

'You disappeared to change your clothes. What else was I supposed to do?'

'You were supposed to make yourself a cup of tea and stay put.'

'Wine seemed a better alternative. I try and avoid caffeine after six. You look nothing like her, you know.'

Kate stiffened. She took a couple of steps into the kitchen with about the same enthusiasm as someone entering a lion's den. This was *her* house and *her* kitchen, and yet he seemed to dominate it with his presence, making her feel as if she needed to ask permission to open the fridge.

'I have no idea what you're talking about.' She helped herself to a glass of wine and took up position at the opposite end of the table. 'And I would rather not get into any of that.'

'Any of what? If you don't know what I'm talking about?'

He slung his long body out of the chair and headed to the fridge, opened the door and peered inside.

'I see you're a very healthy eater,' he said conversationally, helping himself to the bottle of wine and bringing it back to the table, where he proceeded to pour himself another glass. 'Although the box of chocolates is a giveaway of a more… *decadent* nature…'

'If you give me five minutes, I'll go and fetch the file on George.'

'But returning to what I said…' This time his dark eyes were thoughtful, serious. 'And that remark you so adroitly tried to avoid. You're nothing like your mother. I looked at some of the pictures you have framed in your sitting room…'

'You shouldn't have come here and you shouldn't have nosed around…' For a few appalling seconds, Kate felt as though her little world was in the process of being tilted on its axis. 'I should never have told you any of that stuff.'

'Why? Is there something wrong with confiding in other people?'

'Do *you*?' She turned the question right back at him. 'Do *you* run around spilling your guts to all and sundry? What about all those models you go out with? Do you get deep and personal with *them*? Do you hold hands and sob over a bottle of wine while you pour your soul out?'

This was what it felt like to lose control. She had always had control, and now here she was, sitting at her own kitchen table, losing it with a guy who had the power to terminate the career she had so carefully built.

And the worst of it was that she didn't want to retract the accusation.

She was aware of him with every pore of her being. He swamped her. When she breathed she felt that she was breathing in his clean, masculine scent. When she leaned forward she could feel his personality wrap around her like tendrils of ivy.

She felt...*alive*.

But not, she told herself uneasily, *in a good way.* There was nothing about Alessandro Preda that could make her feel *anything* in a good way. She felt alive in a *very, very annoying* way.

'At least you're not apologizing for asking that daring question,' Alessandro drawled.

So she had ditched the shorts and the cropped top, but the jeans and the baggy shirt did nothing to reduce her sex appeal. Now he had seen that body shorn of its camouflage outfits the image was imprinted in his brain with the force of a branding iron.

'And you're right. I *don't* tend to do the personal touchy-feely business with the women I go out with. I can't recall pouring my soul out and sobbing in recent times.' His mouth twitched with amusement. 'In that we're strangely alike. But you wear your defence system on the outside. You cover up from neck to ankle but there's no need. You're not your mother. You may want to make sure you don't follow in her footsteps, but you don't have to dress like a spinster school-teacher to do that.'

'How dare you come here and try and analyze me?' Tears stung the back of her throat but thankfully she was far too reticent a person to allow them access.

'I'm not trying to analyze you,' Alessandro told her in just the sort of gentle voice that she knew might prove her undoing if she let it. 'Don't you feel a little trapped by all the hoops you make yourself jump through?

'I don't feel trapped by anything. This is the life I've chosen to lead. You have no idea what it's like to be…insecure when you're growing up…'

'How do you know that?' Alessandro asked softly.

Her eyes widened. She paused for thought. How *did* she know that? Because of who he was? Rich. Powerful. Confident. *Arrogant.* Those were not the hallmarks of someone whose upbringing had been anything but exemplary. Besides, he was the sole issue of the union of two wealthy families. If you looked him up on the internet—*which she never had*—you would discover that. She had overhead one of the giggly girls from the legal department imparting that titbit one day in the office restaurant. He occupied a stratosphere that was quite unlike hers. Actually, quite unlike most peoples.

'But you were right when you said that we're here to talk about Cape.'

For a minute there Alessandro had felt the pull to trade one set of confidences for another. He didn't know where that had come from, but it wasn't something he was going to give in to. Probably hearing her talk about her mother had naturally led him to think about his own parents. They too lived on the coast—probably not a million miles away from her mother. Small world...

'Of course. I'll just go and fetch the file I've compiled. I've summarized all my findings. I thought it might be easier for you to go through rather than follow the trail piecemeal.'

'Highly efficient, and just what I would expect of you!'

Kate frowned, but before she could rise to the bait he interceded with a grin.

'And, before you jump down my throat, I *wasn't* being sarcastic...'

'I wasn't about to imply that you were.' But she had been. And that made her feel a little uneasy. Either she was as transparent as a pane of glass, which was a bad thing, or else he could read her mind—which was a bad thing.

And what had he meant when he had hinted that it wasn't true that he wouldn't know what it might feel like to have an insecure background?

She felt her pulse race at the thought of him

confiding in her and had to yank herself back to the reality that, when all was said and done, he was her boss and they had nothing in common.

Maybe he was right about that ivory tower, she thought feverishly as she fetched the file and headed back to the kitchen. Not as it applied to her in an office scenario but as it applied to her in a *life* scenario. Maybe she *had* lived life in the safe middle lane for too long. Maybe she *had* detached herself too much from the highs and lows of getting involved with people…with *men*. Maybe that was why she was behaving like this with him: disobeying common sense and flirting with something dangerous…

Flirting with an impossible attraction.

Shoot me in the head first, she thought.

But she had to take a deep, steadying breath before she pushed open the door and stepped inside where, thankfully, he was still in the same place and not snooping through the kitchen drawers and making himself even more at home.

'Would you like some coffee?' she asked politely, and Alessandro raised his eyebrows.

'I don't need sobering up,' he told her drily. 'So no, thank you. Besides, what did I tell you about caffeine after six?'

'Yes, you did say that—but I do remember you helping yourself to several cups of strong black coffee a few months ago, when we were working with George and a couple of others on that deal late into the night...'

'I didn't realize that you had been keeping a watch on what I was eating and drinking...'

God, but she was sexy when she blushed like that and looked away, as though she was in danger of giving away state secrets if she met his eyes. He felt himself stir again, aroused by images that had no place in his head.

He waved his hand for her to hand over her findings and started reading. There wasn't a great deal to get through—less than he had been expecting.

'So all in all,' he said slowly, raising his eyes to hers, 'he hasn't been at it for very long...'

'Which I think is in his favour...'

'We'll have to agree to disagree on that one. The fact is that the man has stolen from me...'

'He must have had a reason.'

'Of course he must have had a reason. Greed. Possibly linked to a debt which had to be paid off. My money is on a gambling debt. Unless you've noticed anything out of the ordinary? Vodka bottles in his desk drawer, perhaps?'

'I can't imagine that George is a gambler,' Kate persisted, thinking furiously, trying to remember if she had noticed anything unusual about his behaviour over the past six months and coming up with nothing. 'And he certainly isn't an alcoholic, if that's what you're implying!'

'How would you know, unless you socialize with him out of work? On a regular basis?'

'He's a good guy.'

'Who has just happened to steal over a hundred grand from me over a five-month period. His halo's slipping slightly, wouldn't you agree? Still, he will have the opportunity to explain his borderline saintly status to a court of impartial jurors, and you are more than welcome to sign on as a character witness.'

'Sometimes—' She swallowed back something she would instantly regret saying and took a deep breath. 'Surely you could at least hear what he has to say before you condemn him and throw away the key…?'

Could he? Well, under any other circumstances there would be no question as to what course of action he would take. There could never be any excuse for fraud. Life was full of people forgiving the idiocy of other people, but in the end idiots deserved the punishment they got. The feckless deserved their fate.

He looked at that earnest face. That beautiful, earnest face. She should be as tough as nails—immune to feelings of empathy given her background. But she wasn't.

She was complex, intriguing, quirky… And all

of this despite the fact that she was so desperate to be just the opposite.

He liked that.

Was there anything wrong with that?

When it came to women he had always been able to have what he wanted. This woman introduced a challenge to his jaded appetite and what was wrong with that? What was wrong if he wanted to explore that just a little bit further?

'I could...' he admitted, watching her carefully. 'Everyone has a story to tell...'

'I know!'

She hazarded a smile, leaned forward.

'You think I'm mad, but I just *know* that George isn't a bad guy. He...he's actually one of the kindest men I've met in my entire life! Although...' She laughed, and the sound was light and infectious, 'Compared to some of the guys I've had the misfortune to meet, thanks to my mother, that's not hard! Not that any of them threatened me in any way,' she added hurriedly, 'but I certainly grew up having first-hand knowledge of how scummy guys can be...'

She smiled shyly at him, marvelling that underneath that forbidding exterior and arrogant self-assurance he might not be quite as unrelenting as she'd thought.

'I'm really glad you're prepared to at least listen to what he has to say.'

Alessandro made a non-committal sound under his breath and smiled at her lazily. 'And wouldn't it be so much fairer if I had this discussion with him face to face? Outside the office? After all, the last thing I want is for the world to see him being marched out in handcuffs...'

'Absolutely,' Kate agreed, delighted at his turn-around. 'That sort of thing would just...*destroy* him...'

'Which is why we are going to fly to Canada and confront him there. Find out just what the hell has been going on. Surprise him, so to speak. But it will be a far less unpleasant surprise than if I do it in the office, with all those curious eyes peering through the glass, people jumping to conclusions and gossiping...'

'Sorry...*we*...?'

'Of course!'

He smiled broadly at her while she stared back, her brain moving sluggishly to compute the message it was receiving.

'You're the one who has influenced me into a decision I would never have otherwise taken. It's only right that you be there when the questions get asked...don't you agree?'

'Well...'

'Congratulations on changing my mind! It's a rare occurrence. I'll get my secretary to book flights out first thing on Monday morning. I take it you have a current passport? Yes? Well, then...' He looked at her with satisfaction. 'That's settled...'

CHAPTER FOUR

Alessandro was waiting for her five days later at the first-class check-in desk at the airport.

Kate spotted him from a mile away. Not hard. He stood out even in a packed terminal, where people were either rushing around frantically or else standing in long queues with blank *How much slower can this line move?* stares.

He was frowning at his smartphone, scrolling through messages, leaning against the counter with a solitary, very expensive holdall on the ground next to him. The picture of understated elegance in cream trousers, a white shirt and a lightweight jacket which he had tossed on top of the holdall.

Having planned on arriving bang on time, if not early, Kate was unavoidably running late and she was hassled.

She thought her neatly pinned-back hair might be unravelling. and her suit and pumps felt stiff and uncomfortable—unsuitable for the heat here in London, never mind abroad. Lord only knew how they would fare on a long-haul flight, but she had been determined to dress appropriately because, crucially, *this wasn't a holiday.*

She had allowed her rules to slip. She had found herself losing her self-control. It was going to be very important that she re-establish that self-control while she was in Toronto on this business trip.

Comfy trousers and a casual cotton jumper with loafers had thus been ruled out as suitable travel gear.

'You're late,' were the first words Alessandro greeted her with as he snapped shut his phone and straightened.

'Traffic. I'm sorry. It would have been quicker for me to have come by tube. But I'm here now, and I hope I haven't kept you waiting too long.' She managed to say all that in a cool, polite voice whilst not actually looking at him at all. 'Have you checked in?'

'I was waiting for you.'

'Is that all the luggage you've brought?' Kate asked incredulously.

Next to his holdall, her suitcase was the size of a small mountain—but they were going for a week, and she hadn't quite known which clothes to take for which occasion. So she had packed to cover every eventuality.

They had found out where George was staying with his wife without actually contacting him for the information—because, as Alessandro had persisted in telling her, the element of surprise would afford him no time to start thinking up fancy stories to cover up what he had done.

Kate hadn't said anything. Poor George. Little did he know what he was in for. Alessandro had assured her that he was prepared to listen, but was he prepared to absolve from blame and forgive?

In the world of Alessandro Preda there was no room for excuses or apologies. If you crossed him in any way retribution would be swift and unforgiving. She could only try and be the restraining hand on his arm, so to speak. It was a minor miracle that he was prepared to listen at all.

'I'm a believer in travelling light,' he said, checking in her suitcase and then taking his time to examine the picture in her passport, while Kate patiently waited for him to return it to her, teeth gritted. 'I take it you're not…?'

'I wasn't sure what to bring with me.'

'So you decided to bring it all? Including the kitchen sink?'

She reddened and mumbled something about it being so much easier for guys, who could fling two things in an overnight bag and disappear abroad for a month.

She might have added that she could count on the fingers of one hand the number of times she had been abroad in her entire life. She wasn't an expert when it came to working out what to pack. Aside from confronting George and ruining his holiday, they would be visiting a potential business opportunity on the outskirts of the city—killing two birds with one stone, so to speak, which was probably partly why Alessandro had chosen to make this trip in the first place.

So, yes, work clothes... But it wasn't really feasible to wear suits in the evenings as well, was it?

Not that she planned on spending a single one of those evenings in *his* company. Not one. She intended to draw some very clear and definite lines. Between nine and five she would be his employee, and after five she would disappear and do her own thing.

So she had stuffed some casual wear in her case as well. Jeans and loose, baggy tops. The woman in the tiny shorts and cropped top with the ponytail was *not* going to make an appearance.

'If I need more clothes,' Alessandro was saying, leading her through customs, handling everything so efficiently that she barely noticed them heading towards the first-class lounge, 'then I can always buy out there. I travel so much that I can be in and out of an airport a lot faster if I don't have to check in any luggage.'

'Hence the holdall?'

'Hence the holdall. Usually I bring something a lot smaller when I'm going to Europe.'

'I can't imagine what could be smaller,' Kate panted, walking fast to keep pace with him. 'A wallet?'

Alessandro chuckled and shot her an appreciative look—which she missed because she was trying to remain composed whilst half running beside him, one hand holding her neat little bun in place, the other dragging a pull-along case which she had stuffed with all sorts of useful reading matter.

'Occasionally,' he drawled, slowing down and veering off to the left, 'a wallet is all a man needs. It can hold a lot more than just banknotes and credit cards...'

'Really? Like what?' Kate retorted sarcastically, getting her breathing back and looking sideways at him. 'A change of outfit? Spare jacket? Pair of shoes?'

He burst out laughing, stopping and looking down at her with an unreadable expression that left her feeling a little dizzy.

'Where have *you* been hiding?'

'Sorry?' She stared back at him, confused.

'This witty, funny woman with the sharp tongue... Where have you been stashing her away? If I'd known she existed I would have taken some time out to try and find her...under the desk, maybe...or behind the coatrack...or in the stationery cupboard...'

Kate couldn't help herself. She blushed and smiled and looked away, and then caught his eyes again. And all the while she was doing that she could feel her heart pick up speed.

There was still laughter in his eyes as he continued to hold her gaze. 'A wallet,' he murmured, his dark eyes suddenly glinting with lazy devilry, 'can hold something that's even more vital than cash or credit cards...'

'What?'

'I'll let you think about it...' He grinned and began walking again, pushing open the glass doors that led to the first-class lounge.

Kate paused and took stock. This was *amazing*. Here, the hustle and bustle of the airport terminal gave way to...well, peace, quiet...glassy counters groaning under the weight of food...men and women on their computers, comfy chairs and sofas...

'Wow.'

Accustomed to all of this, Alessandro took a few seconds to register her expression, and he felt a weirdly heady kick at having been the one to introduce her to the experience.

'So *this* is how the other half live,' she breathed, impressed to death. 'Am I standing out like a sore thumb?'

She looked at him anxiously and he smiled.

'I don't think there's a dress code in opera-tion here,' he told her gently, guiding her forward and flicking their first-class passes to the well-groomed woman behind the polished curved counter.

Actually, there was. The dress code was *expensive*. He felt a sudden surge of protectiveness, which he dismissed as the normal reaction of a boss looking out for his employee. Having her insulted, stared at or criticized in any way was something he would not tolerate.

He ushered her to a long, low sofa, settled her down. When he asked her what she would like to drink he was amused to see her spring to her feet, eyes bright.

'I should do the honours,' she told him seriously. 'You *are* my boss, after all...'

'Of course,' Alessandro murmured. 'What was I thinking?'

So she didn't blend in? He was suddenly contemptuous of all those unspoken rules the seriously wealthy played by. A rich diet of supermodels had blinded him to the realities that everyone else lived with. And, of all people, shouldn't he know that the wealthy had their failings? Didn't always conform?

He frowned, distracted by the rare intrusion of introspection. He came from wealth—had known first-hand its ups and downs, had experienced the frailty of what could be so easily taken for granted. He was secure in his own personal fortune—had made sure of that—but it struck him that he no longer looked outside the box at lifestyles that weren't rich and privileged.

He was accustomed to his rare stratosphere because it was the one everyone he knew inhabited—including the women he dated. Although it had to be said that their passports came via their incredible looks.

She returned five minutes later with two plates heaped with various titbits, from little dainty sandwiches to cream cakes and packets of biscuits.

'I've gone a little mad,' she confessed. 'I know it's not cool to take a bit of everything that's there, but I couldn't resist.'

'You don't have to justify yourself to me, Kate. Take whatever you want. That's what it's there for. I'd bet that half the people here would love to do the same, but some warped sense of wanting to *blend in* and *look cool* stops them.'

Kate breathed a sigh of relief. 'I'm ravenous, anyway.'

'We could have a full breakfast if you'd rather?'

'You're kidding?'

'Perfectly serious. Airlines command fat fares for first-class travellers. Frankly, hot food in their lounges is the very least one can expect.'

'I'm fine.' She reminded herself that she wasn't there to have fun. Work was what was on the agenda—and not of a very pleasant nature either. 'But thank you for the offer.'

She tucked in as delicately as possible whilst noticing that he ate next to nothing.

'You can work if you want to,' she contributed awkwardly. 'You don't have to feel that I need entertaining.'

'I don't.'

She reluctantly looked at the little pile of un-eaten sandwiches on her plate. 'How do you intend to...to confront George? Have you given it much thought? I know you have all the evidence compiled, but are you just going to present him with it in front of his wife?'

'Haven't thought that far ahead.'

'I'd hate him to think that I might have been the one to instigate this whole sorry business,' she admitted. 'Although if I show up at your side I guess that's the first thing he'll think.'

'Why does it matter?' Alessandro dismissed her concern with a careless shrug. 'So he gets the boot and puts it down to you? What's the big deal?'

'The "big deal" is that some of us actually *care* what other people think of them.'

'Why? Will you ever see him again? His family?'

'That's not the point.' She looked at him curiously. 'How can you be so...so cold and detached?'

And he was. Despite the fact that he socialized heavily, dated women by the bucketload if office gossip and the daily tabloids were anything to go by, there was something about Alessandro Preda that remained remote and untouchable.

She shivered. Was that all part and parcel of his incredible appeal?

In the City he was feared as a ruthless competitor. Men and women alike were awed by him. Even here, as she surreptitiously slid her eyes to the side, she could see the way people checked him out. He commanded attention and took it as his right. They all knew he was rich, or else he wouldn't be in a first-class lounge. They only wondered if he was famous—and if so famous, for what?

But, for all the attention he garnered, on some level he didn't *engage*. Why was that? she wondered.

'Trust me…cold and detached are two words that have *never* been used by a woman to describe me…'

And all at once Kate knew what he had been referring to with that little smile curling his lips, when he had told her that wallets held more important stuff than money and credit cards.

Condoms.

A man who could have whatever woman he

wanted always had to be prepared, she thought, with a burst of cynicism.

It was incredible that she had managed to forget just what sort of a person he was. He might be remote, he might be as shallow as a puddle when it came to anything emotional, but he was also witty, intelligent, and when he focused those dark, speculative, brooding eyes on her, all her misgivings floated away like dew on a hot summer morning.

Which didn't change the fact that he was a man who made sure he carried condoms in his wallet—because who knew when some poor good-looking girl might cross his path, hoping for more than just a one-night stand or a one-month fling with a bunch of goodbye roses when she was on her way out?

'Well, this is one woman who's using them now,' Kate said coolly. 'When we've confronted poor George in his hotel room and you've shaken him down and booted him out of your company without a backward glance, will you be able to wipe your hands and walk away without giving him a second thought? Because if you can then you're cold and detached—and it doesn't matter how many adoring fans tell you the opposite.'

From any other woman Alessandro would not have taken this. He had his rules and his boundaries and those were lines that were never crossed.

In truth, he never really even had to lay them down. They were unwritten, unspoken and obeyed without fail.

Kate Watson—who, on the surface, promised to be as non-committal as a plank of wood—chose to disregard every single one of those boundary lines, and her rampant disobedience intrigued him and he didn't quite know why.

Maybe it was the dichotomy between what she strove to conceal and what she was lured into revealing against her better judgement.

He might not be involved with her on a personal level, but there was something in her that aroused his interest.

'I expect you're going to remind me that it's not my place to voice opinions about you or what you do...' she muttered in a half-hearted apology.

'We're going to be in each other's company for a week. If you have something to say then you might as well get it off your chest. I don't think I can face your constant disapproval. And I'm guessing from those pursed lips that you *do* disapprove of me?'

'I... No, of course I don't...' Her voice fell away.

'Of course you do. You have opinions on the type of person I am, and admiration isn't one of them. That's something you've decided you'll leave to those adoring fans of mine.'

Hot colour crawled up into her cheeks. *Pursed*

lips. She was a woman with *pursed lips* and *disapproval* and *starchy suits*. He was *fun*. And she was *the schoolmarm who always rained on his parade*.

Except it wasn't *fun* when there was some poor, deluded hopeful woman at the receiving end, was it?

'I have a lot of admiration for your business acumen,' she said stiffly. 'They say that everything you touch turns to gold. That's quite an achievement. I think it takes a lot to be a guy who builds all the businesses and it's something quite different from the guy who services them. You're the guy who builds the businesses.'

'Not exactly *adoring*, though, is it…?' he mused. 'When it comes to accolades…?'

He enjoyed the way she blushed. It was something he had never noticed before. Like a wayward horse tugging at its reins, his mind broke its leash and zoomed back to the picture of her in those shorts, long legs going on for ever, full breasts bouncing braless in that small top.

Great body sternly kept under wraps because she had learned lessons from having a mother who was too ready to flaunt hers.

Had she ever flaunted her body for a man?

'I don't have to be a member of your fan club to appreciate that you're talented at what you do.'

She wanted to tell him that this was hardly appropriate conversation, but she suspected that he didn't give a damn what was appropriate and what wasn't. He did what he wanted to do because he could.

If she annoyed him too much she would probably find herself next to George on a trip to never-never land.

'But when it comes to anything that isn't work-related your admiration levels drop off sharply—am I right?' Her face was averted and he absently appreciated the fine delicacy of her profile. He had a sudden urge to release her long chestnut-brown hair from its ridiculous clips and pins.

'I suppose I have different standards to you when it comes to relationships,' she said eventually, when the silence was threatening to overwhelm her. She wasn't looking at him, but she could feel his dark eyes boring into the side of her face.

What was this all about? He didn't give a hoot what she thought about his personal life. Maybe he was irritated because she was being a little more forthcoming than he was used to, but her outspokenness probably amused him.

She was providing him with a different taste sensation—why not try it?

'And tell me what those standards are...'

Kate swung to look at him and discovered that he was leaning towards her, far too close for comfort.

Dark, dark eyes with ridiculously long eyelashes clashed with hers and the breath caught in her throat. She inched back, furious with herself for feeling uncomfortable in his presence, for letting him *get to her*, when she had given herself a stern talk about all that nonsense before she had left her house.

'I...'

'You're not going to dry up on me now, are you, Kate? When you've come this far?'

And just how had she managed to do that? she wondered. One minute they were striding through an airport and the next minute she had launched into a personal attack on his moral standards. Or as good as!

Trapped by her own idiocy, she frantically tried to think of a clever way to change the conversation, but he was waiting for her to say something. And not a sudden commentary on the weather or the state of the economy. No such luck. Why would he rescue her from her hideous discomfort when he could get a kick from pinning her to the wall and watching her wriggle like a worm on a hook?

'I don't approve of men who...*use* women. Maybe that's the wrong word,' she corrected hastily. 'I mean I don't approve of men who slide in and out of relationships, trying them on for size and then discarding the ones that don't quite fit.'

'And what about women who try men on for size?'

'That doesn't happen.'

'No?' He raised his eyebrows in a cool question. 'Ever had a boyfriend, Kate?'

'Of course I have!' she said hotly. 'And I don't see what that has to do with anything!'

'Where is he now?'

'I beg your pardon?'

'Where is this wonder guy now?' He peered around him, as if at any moment the man in question would stride out from where he had been hiding behind a computer terminal.

'We... It finished...'

'Ah.' Alessandro sat back and linked his fingers lightly on his lap. 'So it didn't work out?'

'No, it didn't,' Kate said uncomfortably.

'Was it a case of him using you ruthlessly before tossing you aside on the discarded heap?'

'No!' she cried, as flustered as a witness sitting in the box, being picked apart by the prosecution.

'Well, what happened, in that case?' And now his tone had changed. Very subtly. Because he'd discovered that he was curious about this mystery guy who hadn't chucked her on his discards pile. 'And don't think about launching into a little sermon about it being none of my business. You don't seem to have too many qualms about speaking your mind, so you can answer one or two questions of your own.'

'We broke up.' She shrugged and tore her eyes away from his lean, aggressive face. 'The timing was wrong,' she admitted grudgingly. 'I was very busy. I wasn't in the right place to fully cultivate the relationship the way it deserved to be cultivated…'

'Ah…so an amicable parting of ways…?'

Kate could have thought of other ways of describing their inevitable split. *Amicable* didn't feature on the list.

'So here's the thing,' he said, voice as smooth as silk and yet razor-sharp. 'You seem to be under the impression that every relationship that doesn't end in a walk up the aisle is a relationship that involves one person using the other. But life's not like that. Yes, it may have been so for your mother, but your mother was a certain type of personality. Your mother—and I'm no expert on this—may have been searching for something, and the only way she could conduct her search was by offering what she had and hoping it got picked by the right kind of guy…'

'You're right. You *don't* know my mother.'

'Maybe your mother was fundamentally insecure,' he carried on relentlessly. 'But that doesn't mean that everyone is like her. She's not the benchmark.'

'I never said she was.'

'No?'

'I should never have said anything,' she breathed resentfully. 'It's awful when you tell someone something and they then proceed to use it against you like in a court of law.'

But didn't he have a point? She refused to concede that he did, but her conscience nagged in a way it never had before. He had stripped her of her convenient black-and-white approach and she didn't want that. It was easier to set a course when you weren't distracted by grey areas and murky questions.

'It's not about the outcome,' she muttered in a driven voice. 'It's about the intent.'

'Explain.'

'I don't want to be having this conversation.' She gazed at the tepid coffee in her cup and wished she had something to fiddle with. 'Maybe we ought to find out whether we should be boarding. Or something.'

'They'll call us when it's time for us to board the plane. Relax.'

She was as tense as a bowstring, her body rigid. So much emotion contained behind that bland exterior. He reached out and brushed his finger against the soft skin on the underside of her wrist and she tensed.

And *he* tensed.

Electric. Unexpected. A high-voltage charge that suddenly ran between them.

He withdrew his hand quickly. 'You initiate conversations,' he said coolly, 'and when the going gets a little tricky you back away because you're too scared to carry on. Weren't you ever taught to finish what you start?'

The lazy teasing had gone, wiped out by that ferocious assault on his senses when he had casually touched her. Watching and speculating was one thing. But what he had felt just then, when he had briefly touched her…

It had felt like a loss of control. For a couple of seconds he had been knocked back by a reaction he had not expected. Curiosity had stoked his libido, but now…now he felt something as powerful as a depth charge. The shock of the unexpected jacked his responses into full alert. For once, toying with the idea of a woman in his bed seemed a dangerous adventure not to be undertaken.

'Okay…' Kate surreptitiously rubbed her wrist where his finger had been. 'If you really want to know, there's a difference between starting a relationship in the hope that it'll develop into something and starting a relationship knowing that it's going to crash and burn when you decide it's time to move on.'

'And I'm a crash-and-burn guy…?'

She shrugged and he stared her down, his dark eyes cool, his expression unreadable.

Was he storing away everything she said to be used at a later date? Did he even care one way or another *what* she said? She decided that, no, he probably didn't. He wasn't the kind of guy who would tolerate personal comments on his moral choices. She couldn't picture any woman sitting him down with a cup of tea and sharing her opinions on his ethics and his principles. They might have a rant when he chucked them over for a new model, but that was different.

Yet here he was now, waiting for her to say something. If he didn't care about her opinions he wouldn't be allowing her this leeway. Would he?

'Sort of… I guess… It's not for me to say…'

'Easy to make assumptions, isn't it?' he said softly. 'You criticized *me* for making assumptions about how your background influenced you…yet here you are… A bit hypocritical, wouldn't you say?'

The question hung in the air between them. Suddenly it felt as though they were the only two people sitting here. Background noise—not that there was much of that—faded, until she could almost hear the beating of her own heart.

It had been easy to tell herself that she could redefine the lines between them. Sitting here, she couldn't understand how those good intentions had been swept aside so fast and so completely.

'If you can't take the heat,' Alessandro drawled, 'then you should stay out of the kitchen. You think it's okay to offer your opinions on what you imagine my personal life is like…? Well, it's a two-way street…'

He beckoned across a young girl who was on the hunt for empty plates and glasses and asked her to fetch him a cup of black coffee, and all the while his eyes remained fastened on Kate's flushed face.

'But I'm glad you brought this up,' he continued, obviously not getting the vibes she was transmitting, 'because, like I said, a week of constant silent disapproval isn't what I need…'

'I didn't *have* to come,' Kate muttered.

'But here you are. And, incidentally, you actually *did* have to come. You had to come because I requested it. So, now we're having this cosy little chat, let me fill you in on your misconceptions. I *don't* pick women up and drop them, having led them up the garden path. I don't make promises I have no intention of fulfilling in exchange for sex.'

Kate stared mutinously at the ground, wishing it would do her a favour and open up and swallow her.

She was being chastised. Like a misbehaving kid in a classroom.

'Trust me—I don't have to do that.'

Coffee was brought to him and Kate noticed the way the young girl half curtseyed and stared at him, goggle-eyed. He might make noises about not wanting to be treated like royalty, and laugh because maybe he really did mean it, but he *was* treated like royalty.

'So you don't leave any broken hearts behind you?' she finally asked, prompted into filling the silence.

He looked at her thoughtfully.

'Maybe I do,' he mused. 'But through no fault of my own.'

Kate's mouth fell open. Talk about ditching responsibility! Her face must have revealed what was going through her head, but this time he relaxed, sipped the coffee that had been brought to him and smiled.

'I don't want commitment and I never pretend that I do,' he said, and she bit down hard on the ready retort rising to her lips. 'I lay my cards on the table from the start.'

'And what would those cards happen to be?' Kate asked politely. She thought that they probably came from the same deck that all commitment-phobes used.

'No strings attached. I tell them from the outset that I'm in it for fun. I give them the opportunity to walk away.'

How considerate.

'No sleepovers…no cosy nights in in front of the telly…no knick-knacks in the bathroom…'

'That's a lot of rules,' Kate said truthfully. 'And then what happens?'

'What do you mean?' Alessandro frowned in puzzlement, because how much clearer could he get with his explanation?

'What if some of the rules get broken? I mean, what if one of your dates decides that she'd rather stay in than go out. But, no… I suppose those supermodel types love the camera, so why would they ever want to do something as boring as *staying in*…?'

Alessandro grinned but didn't say anything. He didn't have to. Why would any woman want to go out when they had the option of staying in a bed with *him*? Kate could read that clearly from his wicked grin.

'My rules don't get broken,' he murmured with soft assurance. 'And if they do then it spells the end of a relationship. And now that we've cleared that up…' He leaned forward to flip open his laptop, which had been resting on the table in front of them.

Now that he had cleared that up she was dismissed—along with her opinions.

CHAPTER FIVE

IT WASN'T THE MOST relaxed of trips, even though it should have been. The first-class service was faultless. There seemed to be no end to the smiling girls waiting at the ready to bring whatever they were told to bring. They were, literally, primed to jump to attention. People paid a fortune—and they didn't just get hot breakfasts in the first-class lounges. The bowing and scraping followed them onto the plane.

Kate had been on a one-week holiday with her mother three years previously. They had flown to Ibiza for a few days of sun and the flight over had been cramped and unpleasant. The airline staff had been abrupt and indifferent and it had been a relief to land and get off.

On this flight she had endless leg room. The seat could be transformed into a bed. There was champagne and wine and the food was of fine-dining standard.

But she shouldn't have worn a suit. The pumps she could dispense with, but the skirt was horribly uncomfortable. Grey jogging bottoms had been thoughtfully provided in a sanitised plastic bag, along with a matching jumper, but she couldn't bring herself to wear either.

The only saving grace was that Alessandro worked and dozed, leaving her to get on with the business of dreading the week ahead.

There was a lot to dread. High on the list was the fact that she could give herself a million stern lectures on keeping her distance but none of those words of wisdom counted for anything—because he seemed to have the power to seduce her into whatever conversation he happened to want at the time.

She could wave the folder she had on George in front of his handsome face, but if he wasn't in the mood to get down to business then he just...*didn't*.

And something about him *propelled* her into speech. The hatefully arrogant man could just tilt his head to one side, direct that devastating half smile on her and off she would go, blabbering on about stuff that didn't concern him and pouring out confidences that she never shared with anyone.

Then he would grow bored and she would be dismissed—just like that.

If in the space of a few days and some snatched conversations she had managed to tell him about her insecure upbringing and how that had made her feel, not to mention her thoughts on men like him, then what was the week ahead going to bring?

And then there was the uncomfortable question of the way she couldn't seem to stop herself from *looking* at him—and not in the harmless way an employee was supposed to look at her boss. Nothing about what he aroused in her felt *appropriate*.

What was *that* all about? Was it because she had been so careful to put things into boxes—to put *men* into boxes—that the first time one had slipped through the net, she had not had the necessary weaponry to deal with the intruder?

That calmed her. It was easy to picture him as an intruder, muscling his way past 'Do Not Trespass' signs, making inroads into places he had no right to be.

She could deal with intruders. Even metaphorical ones. So she might have been caught off guard? That didn't mean that she was doomed to being caught off guard whenever she happened to be in his company. She might be inexperienced but she wasn't a complete idiot!

She was in a better frame of mind by the time the plane began taxiing down to land.

'Good flight?' he asked as everyone began to stand in preparation for disembarking. 'You look a little...rumpled. Didn't I question your choice of outfit? Why didn't you wear the comfy clothes provided? Or didn't you locate them…?'

'I had a very good flight,' Kate answered serenely. 'It was relaxing. I read my book, watched a couple of movies, dozed…and as a matter of fact I'm very comfortable with my choice of clothing.'

The damn man looked as fresh as a daisy—all bright-eyed and bushy-tailed and ready for what was waiting for them in Toronto.

She didn't dare glance down at her skirt, which would be horribly creased—a suitable companion to her shirt, which was also horribly creased. She wondered whether it was physically possible for a face to look creased as well. If it was, then she would bet that hers did.

But her smile was wide and bright.

'It beats travelling cattle class,' she volunteered, making sure not to watch as he hoisted his bag down from the overhead locker, as well as her own pull-along. 'I guess I should make the most of it. I don't see it happening again any time soon.'

'You aim too low.'

Alessandro looked down at her as they began the process of disembarking. Her neat bun was disobeying orders from above and staging a rebellion. Tendrils had escaped and she had tried to push them back into position without much success. She looked as though she had travelled prepared to step out of the plane straight into a board meeting, but had been dragged through a hedge somewhere along the way. *Cute.*

'I like to aim for what I can reasonably achieve,' she replied primly, stepping past him and out into the sweltering summer heat.

She felt his warm breath on her neck as he leant towards her from behind.

'Repeat. You aim too low. Reasonable achievements are for the unadventurous.'

'That's me,' she said sharply, half turning towards him. She spun back round and heard him chuckle behind her.

She had no idea what to expect of Toronto, having never travelled further afield than Ibiza, but whatever lay in store, it would flash past in style—because they'd cleared customs and outside there was a stretch limo waiting for them.

'Is this another *wow* moment?' Alessandro cupped her elbow with his hand and ushered her into the long, luxurious, totally over-the-top car.

There was lazy amusement in his voice.

When she had been feverishly writing him off as an intruder, who could be locked out with just a little bit of will power, she had been dealing with a cardboard cut-out in her head. Which was what she wanted him to be. An arrogant, obnoxious, ruthless cardboard cut-out.

Unfortunately the second he opened his mouth,

her brain rebelled against categorizing him because he had far too many layers.

'It's just a car,' she returned politely.

It wasn't. Just a car was something small that took you from A to B, and fingers crossed it didn't decide to break down en route. At least, that would be the kind of car she would probably buy in a year or two.

'I'm not impressed because I don't see the point of something this big. I mean, you can't nip down to the supermarket in it, can you?'

'Good point. However you *can* help yourself to a glass of whisky from the handy little bar… Care for a drink?'

Kate shook her head. The last thing she needed was to start relaxing into yet another dangerous conversation with him.

She looked through the window, her whole body aware of him next to her, lazily lounging against the door, his long legs spread slightly apart.

'Have you been here before?' she asked eventually, turning to him, her body pressed against the door.

'If you'd paid attention to those reports on the company we're going to try and fit in while we're here, you'd have seen that I was here less than six months ago. Don't tell me you haven't scoured the file? I'll be bitterly disappointed.'

Kate cleared her throat. 'You enjoy doing that, don't you?'

'Enjoy doing what?'

'Winding me up.'

'Is that what I was doing? I thought I was paying you a backhanded compliment, as a matter of fact. You're such a professional that I expected you to have scoured that file from front to back and memorized everything in it.'

'I glanced through it. I wasn't aware that I was going to be actively involved in the acquisition.'

'Why wouldn't you be?'

'Because it's quite a sizeable…er…I just thought that perhaps someone a bit higher up the pecking order would be put in charge…'

'I don't see how that's going to be possible,' Alessandro mused speculatively, 'when George will be busy packing up his belongings for the big goodbye. You waxed lyrical about your ambitions…'

'Of *course* I'm ambitious.' She automatically fell into familiar terrain. As long as they were talking about work then she was comfortable, and repeating her hopes for her career was a damn sight safer than getting lost in a personal conversation with him.

'Yes—you need to build financial security to protect you because you lacked it when you were growing up…'

'I want to get on,' she amended through gritted teeth.

'The work you did for me last week on those files I dropped off for you…good job…'

Kate flushed with pleasure. 'You mean it?'

'I can see why Cape decided that you had what it took to fast-track you. Mind you, I'm thinking he was busy directing his attention elsewhere, so it helped that you were so quick. You could pick up any slack.' He grinned. 'And before you launch into a defence of the hapless George, I have a proposition for you…'

'What?'

'Instead of recruiting from outside for a replacement for Cape, I am considering promoting you. Of course you won't qualify for Cape's vacated post, but you'll effectively be hoisted a couple of steps up the career ladder. You will be responsible for bigger accounts, and to alleviate any bad feeling with the people you work with I will reorganize the team. There will be a greater distribution of more responsible tasks and I'll bring in a few lower down the scale to be trained up. Effectively, you and your team will all benefit…'

'I…I couldn't…' Guilt swept over her. 'Poor George finds himself without a job, thrown on the scrap heap, and to top it all off I step into his shoes. I would feel like I was dancing on someone's grave.'

Alessandro frowned. 'You're being melodramatic. No one's dancing on anyone's grave. A vacancy will arise with his departure...it makes complete sense...'

'It might make sense, but it doesn't make it *right*...'

'He leaves and I either recruit from outside, with all the attendant hassle of training someone up, or I promote from within the company—and you're the obvious choice. You want financial security? This will lever you a couple of rungs up the security ladder.'

'It's not black and white like that!'

'Fine. *You* can get lost in the grey blurry bits, but it's pretty black and white from where I'm standing. Furthermore, would you deny your colleagues a golden opportunity to advance their careers because you're so concerned about a guy who didn't seem to care very much when it came to defrauding the company that's treated him very well for countless years?'

'You could still do something for them...I don't have to be part of the equation...'

'No deal. You accept the whole package or you don't. Simple as that. Think about it...'

'I...' Could she deny the people who worked alongside her their chance of getting pay rises? Of going further with their careers?

'Of course this would not be with immediate effect,' Alessandro said, watching her carefully. 'There would be a slow transfer of duties and when I'm reassured that you're up to the increased workload, you will be given a new title… and a suitable pay rise to reflect that. See this as my having faith in your abilities and not as twisting the knife in someone else's back. If any knife-twisting has gone on, it's been done by Cape to himself. He dug his grave the minute he decided to start embezzling.'

'I—I'm pleased that you have faith in my abilities,' Kate stammered. 'But…' She sighed. 'We don't know what will happen about George. We haven't…you know…heard what he has to say yet…'

'Don't really have to,' Alessandro told her gently. 'I could humour you by pretending that I give a damn about his explanation, but in my book theft is theft. My only concern is how he will be rewarded for his misdoings…'

'So this trip is…pointless…?'

'This trip is about you being on an essential learning curve when it comes to handling awkward situations. There's no room for grey areas or indecision. And whether you accept the promotion I'm offering you or allow your guilt to get the better of your good sense, you should know one thing: the higher up the ladder you climb, the more important it is for you to know how to do that.'

'In other words I have to become as ruthless as…as…?'

'As me?'

'I guess I believe there are other ways of…of…'

'There aren't.'

'You're so cut-throat…'

'Life has a curious way of shaping our responses.'

Kate looked at him and wondered what he meant by that. Was it just a general remark, or were there factors in his life that had made him the way he was? He was beyond rich, beyond powerful and beyond good-looking—and yet he moved from woman to woman with no intention of settling down. Why *was* that?

What it was, she told herself sternly, was *none of her business*.

'Of course…' Alessandro moved on smoothly. 'Before you accept your brand-new shiny job promotion—and I know you will because it would be stupid not to, and you're not stupid—there's something I should ask you…'

'What's that?'

'How reliable do you think you will be in this new role? You don't seem to object to putting in overtime in the steady climb upwards, but will that become difficult for you when and if you're given extra responsibilities and overtime ceases to be a choice and becomes a necessity? No, don't answer that. But think about it and we will discuss it over dinner. The back of a cab—even a very long cab—is no place to have this conversation.'

'Dinner?'

What dinner? What was wrong with room service in their separate rooms and a career discussion over a cup of coffee in the morning?

'It's all we'll be able to do with what remains of the day.' Alessandro was irked at the look of horror that had flashed across her face. 'We both *do* have to eat,' he said coolly.

'Yes, but I thought that I might just grab something in my room and hit the sack early. It's been a long day.'

'Well, you'll have to rethink your plans.'

'Of course.'

'And I trust your *entire* wardrobe isn't comprised of a selection of starchy suits…?'

'What difference does it make?' Kate asked tightly.

'It's not a working meal.'

Control. Yes, he understood. You didn't have to be a genius to join the dots. Her background had made her the sort of woman who felt a driving need to impose control in every aspect of her life. She controlled her appearance, she controlled her hair, she controlled her reactions, controlled her emotions. She was so serious that it was sometimes hard to believe that she was actually in her twenties. All over the world there were grannies out and about having more fun than her. And he wasn't used to women looking appalled at the thought of spending five minutes in his company.

'You can relax in my company for five seconds, Kate.'

Frankly, she thought she already had—and it hadn't been a good idea. 'Right…'

'You *could* sound more convinced.' Irritation had crept into his voice. 'We're here.'

She hadn't even noticed the stretch limo slowing. She had missed most of the trip because her attention had been exclusively focused on the man sitting next to her. So much for dispelling the intruder by getting a grip.

She looked around her and saw a city that was like any other—although there was something more peaceful and less frantic about it than London. The hotel they were approaching was, as she might have expected, the last word in expensive, from its imposing facade to the doormen waiting to relieve the wealthy visitors of their baggage, eager to make sure that they did absolutely nothing for themselves if it could be helped.

The foyer was bustling with visitors, coming and going. Next to them Kate felt the inadequacy of her carefully chosen but now creased outfit. She didn't blend in. Even some of the younger people in jeans and tee shirts managed to look staggeringly designer-casual, as though they had randomly plucked something out of the wardrobe and yet succeeded in looking effortlessly *cool*.

For a few rebellious seconds she wished that she hadn't tied her hair back—wished that she hadn't worn a knee-length drab skirt and a sensible blouse. She wished, for the first time in her life, that she had taken a page out of her mother's book and made the most of her assets.

She frowned. Alessandro had accused her of being a hypocrite and she had predictably reacted by hitting the roof—because who was he to pass judgement on her? Yet, wasn't she?

If she'd seen life in exactly the same black-and-white way that he did wouldn't she have worn more comfortable clothes for the flight over? Brought more to wear than stuff that could only be labelled as *excruciatingly businesslike*...? Had a wardrobe that actually contained clothes a girl her age would wear? She was so scared of emulating her mother that she had veered off in completely the opposite direction, ignoring the fact that there was always a middle ground.

No wonder he was so entertained by her! No wonder he got a kick out of winding her up! She played straight into his hands by trying to control everything she said and did—way more than the occasion demanded.

Yet he *had* seen her in relaxed mode, she

thought with a twinge of discomfort. And whilst that would have been nothing for him, because he was used to seeing far more beautiful women wearing a lot less, it had been something for her. She had felt exposed and vulnerable. Stupid.

She surfaced to find that she was being led out of the foyer and towards a bank of lifts up to her hotel room—which would give her welcome relief from her thoughts.

She was a lot less relieved when they were shown to the same door, which was flung open to reveal an absolutely enormous suite. She stared at it in horror.

'What's this?' She remained firmly planted in the doorway, only shifting to allow the porter inside, watching with her arms folded until he was dispatched and the only occupants of the vast room were Alessandro and herself.

Alessandro looked around, as though noticing his surroundings for the first time.

She was so predictable in her reactions. Dismay at the prospect of being in his company, horror at imagining dinner with him, and now downright shrieking tension, barely kept in check, at the idea that this vast suite might be a shared situation.

Was it any wonder that he couldn't seem to stop himself from goading her?

Especially when, as it was now, the colour

staining her cheeks looked just so unbelievably appealing?

As was her half-opened mouth, her flashing eyes, and the way her pink tongue had sneaked out to moisten her lips...

'It's a room, Kate,' he said, in the patient voice of someone explaining the obvious. 'Hotels tend to have them. It's a must when it comes to attracting potential guests.'

'Ha-ha.' She wasn't budging. She could feel her pulse racing as she craned her neck from her position by the door to try and ascertain just what the situation was regarding sleeping arrangements.

He couldn't possibly expect them to share *a bedroom*, could he? No. No way.

As if reading her thoughts, and reluctantly deciding to put her out of her misery, he said without looking at her, strolling towards the huge bay window to gaze idly outside, 'No need to panic. This is where I'll be staying.'

He turned to face her and saw her visibly relax.

'I asked my secretary to book two adjoining rooms. It wasn't a necessity, but I thought it might be more convenient if this deal kicks off and we find ourselves having to work late. I only realized when I read through the confirmation that my instructions were taken a little too literally...'

He took his time walking towards a door which she hadn't noticed and flung it open.

'You're in there… Actually, if you'd looked at the bedroom you would have noticed that your case is nowhere in evidence. You could have spared yourself your giddy meltdown.'

'I was *not* having a *giddy meltdown*… I was just curious as to… Well…'

'You may have your opinions on my relationships with women…' Alessandro's voice was cool and hard '…but I draw the line at sharing a bedroom with one of my employees when we're on business…'

And when we're not?

Kate shoved aside the immediate thought that sprang into her head on the back of his remark. She walked towards the door and peered into a suite that was almost as big as the one in which she was standing.

'And, before you ask, yes, there's a lock on the interconnecting door—so you'll be quite safe should I find myself accidentally trying to sleep-walk into your bedroom.'

His voice left her in no doubt that that was the last thing he would consider doing. There was laughter just below the surface and she flushed. *She* might be having a hard time disassociating the sex-on-legs guy from the guy who actually paid her salary, but that was because of her own overactive imagination.

'In that case,' she said stiffly, 'I think I'll

freshen up...have a bath.' She looked at him. 'I wonder whether it might not be a better idea for us to continue our discussion about my job in the morning. When we're more alert.'

'It's not even seven-thirty in the evening,' Alessandro said drily. 'I think I'm alert enough to focus. And in the morning we can both look forward to a fun-packed full day tracking down our adventurous crook. So...' He looked at his Rolex and then back at her as she waited, ready to sprint to safety. 'I can either come and get you in an hour, or so you can meet me in the bar downstairs...which would you rather?'

'I'll meet you,' Kate muttered.

'Fine. In an hour sharp.' He grinned. 'You can scuttle off and have your bath now...'

Scuttle.

Horrible word. *Scuttle* was the sort of thing timid little creatures did to get away from danger. Admittedly Alessandro might easily be classed as a dangerous species—at least to her peace of mind—but she had never particularly considered herself a timid little creature.

She had had to develop a tough streak just to get though most of her childhood. In addition to her mother's guilelessly flamboyant jobs, her shocking naivety when it came to the opposite sex and her casual disregard for most aspects of parenting, Kate had also had to be on standby for her mother when her heart had inevitably got broken.

In the framework of things, being timid was a luxury she had never been able to afford.

But was that how Alessandro saw her? If so, wouldn't that come into play when it came to sealing the deal on any job promotion for her? Who wanted someone *timid* handling important accounts and clients?

The clothes she had packed all fell into the category of *timid*. When she had chosen what to take she had made sure to pack stuff that conveyed the right message—she was a working woman on business. A few less formal things had been brought for those evenings that she had intended spending on her own, discovering the city at her own pace and without her challenging boss for company.

Prospects on that particular front now looked anything but sunny. Overcast with the threat of downpours might be more like it.

She took her time enjoying her bath, absently marvelling at the size of the bathroom, and then, with a sigh, opted for a variation on the eternal suit. The navy skirt was, like all her work skirts, knee-length, but instead of a white blouse she chose a red one. And after a lot of hesitation decided against the bun—because she could already visualize those mocking dark eyes taking in the ensemble and having a laugh at her expense.

It took her a while to find the bar. The hotel was enormous, with extensive shopping within it and several dining areas. Eventually, however, she was directed to one of the less casual bars, which was where she expected he would be. Relaxing over a whisky and soda and amusing himself with various scenarios involving George and his dismissal.

Sure enough, he was there, nursing a drink, although it looked like wine instead of whisky.

He glanced at her as soon as she began heading in his direction.

He had changed out of his travelling gear into a pair of cream trousers, an open-necked pale shirt and some loafers. He looked completely at ease—which had the perverse effect of making her feel totally out of place.

She had brought her tablet, which she placed on the table before sitting down.

'What's that for?'

Alessandro poured her a glass of wine before she could tell him that she wasn't going to be drinking.

'Have you decided that you'd rather watch a movie than talk to me?'

Instantly flustered, Kate adjusted the tablet and then sat back, hands on her lap. 'I thought I'd take notes on it rather than on paper,' she told him.

'We're having an informal chat.' Alessandro finished his wine, and before he could top up his glass someone materialized and did it for him before subsiding back into the background. 'I'm not dictating terms and conditions.'

'Yes, I know that. But...'

'No matter. If it makes you happy to busy yourself on a tablet then who am I to tell you otherwise? I thought we'd eat here. It's less formal than one of the hotel restaurants and it saves us the trouble of venturing out... Unless you'd rather do a bit of city exploring...? See what's out there...?'

He waited for a heated negative to that idea—which, predictably, he got.

Did she ever let her hair down? he wondered. Aside from when she was closeted away in her house, safe in her territory, where no one could see her? Unless they unexpectedly dropped by and refused to go away without being invited inside... What did she do *for fun*? Did she have any? Or was that an alien concept to be avoided at all costs?

Curiosity niggled away at him, and he wasn't sure whether he was impatient with that, exasperated or invigorated—because curiosity and women was a combination that didn't occur in his life.

His dark eyes lazily fastened to her face, he summoned the same guy who had leapt to refill his glass and somehow managed to convey a request for menus without actually saying anything.

Kate watched this interplay between power and subservience, unsettled but fascinated.

'I sincerely hope you've brought something else to wear tomorrow, Kate. It's boiling here at this time of year...'

'I'll be fine,' Kate said airily.

'Sure? Because if you've brought those shorts of yours then feel free to wear them. They'd be far more appropriate, given the weather. The food here's excellent,' he carried on, as menus were placed in front of them. 'I stayed here the last time I was in Toronto and I couldn't fault the food. Or the service.'

'They're very obliging,' Kate said politely. 'I guess it's the least you'd expect, considering what you're probably paying...'

Alessandro grinned. 'A bit like the service and the hot meals in the first-class lounge...? Touché...'

'I don't suppose you ever slum it...'

'I try and avoid that. Why? Have I been missing out?'

At the prospect of another detour into a personal conversation she didn't want—one she would have to manoeuvre through with the adroitness of someone walking in a minefield—Kate brought the talk firmly round to business and the reason why she was sitting opposite him in the first place. In a darkened bar. Knees practically touching under the table. Chilled wine in front of them. She inched her knees to one side and hoped he hadn't noticed.

'You mentioned in the car on the way here that there was something you wanted to talk to me about in connection with this job promotion… that's why I've brought my tablet, as a matter of fact. I thought it might be an idea to make some notes on the various responsibilities I'll be taking on board.'

'Ah, down to business straight away…'

Kate reddened, resenting the way that simple observation made her feel instantly like a bore. A bore in a semi-suit.

'Good idea. You're right. We'll probably both need our beauty sleep if tomorrow's going to be a long day.'

Kate searched his face for typical Alessandro irony but he returned her gaze seriously. Not that she believed *he* needed to go to sleep at this hour. She doubted he needed much sleep at all. Maybe even none. He struck her as the sort of guy who could just keep going…and going…and going… taking the occasional power nap while the rest of the world collapsed, exhausted, in his wake.

And he'd be able to do that whilst still managing to look, frankly, drop-dead gorgeous.

They both ordered something light from the menu and then she nervously gulped down a generous mouthful of wine and looked to him to carry on the conversation. He didn't.

'Yes...' she returned feebly at last. 'So...'

'So here's the thing, Kate.'

He leaned forward, suddenly all business, and she inched back in the chair, taking the wine glass with her.

'If you recall, I expressed some concern that you might find the hours attached to your new role a little tedious if you're forced to do them... and that's something we should clear up right here and right now before going any further...'

He really had the most amazing eyelashes. He hadn't shaved, and there was a shadowy stubble on his chin that also looked pretty amazing.

Kate tore her eyes away from both those *amazing* features and focused on him with a slight frown.

'There's nothing to clear up,' she told him crisply. 'I have no problem working long hours, if required. I one hundred per cent realize that that's all part and parcel of any job that entails responsibility.'

Alessandro made a non-committal sound under his breath and sat back, pushing his chair away from the table so that he could cross his legs. He looked at her long and thoughtfully.

'What about your personal life? Not to put too fine a point on it, I wouldn't like to find that I've promoted you and you're not up to the challenge because there's some guy in the background, waiting for you to return home to cook his dinner...'

'That won't be the case,' Kate responded hotly. 'Firstly, there's no man in the background—and secondly, even if there was, I certainly wouldn't expect him to be a demanding kind of guy who wants his dinner cooked by me! In fact the reason I broke up with my last boyfriend—' She clamped shut her mouth and stared at him, aghast.

He returned her stare, unperturbed.

'Those sort of demanding men are to be avoided at all costs,' he murmured softly. 'I'm taking it that the boyfriend wanted more than you were prepared to give...? Hence he was given the heave-ho...?'

'I... It was a very busy time for me... I...' She cleared her throat and attempted to recover her lost composure. 'So you needn't fear that my mind won't be completely on the job.'

'I'm relieved. Although,' he mused, 'I sympathize. I guess he must have been an important person in your life, because you did tell me that you don't believe in transitory relationships...'

'It didn't work out,' Kate told him firmly, as she frantically sought an exit from the conversation. 'I don't dwell on the past.'

'Very wise. Although you *do* allow it to influence certain aspects of your life. For instance, your dress code.'

At which point she decided that the next thing she would do, just as soon as she got the chance, would be to wipe that smirk off his face by making a point of showing him just how much it did *not* affect her dress code.

One slip-up—*one* slip up and the wretched man thought that he knew everything there was to know about her.

'And now that we've settled that,' she said calmly, 'maybe you could let me know how you plan on handling tomorrow...?'

CHAPTER SIX

KATE SPENT A restless night, even though she'd checked and double-checked and, just for good measure, triple-checked that the interconnecting door was firmly locked.

She didn't expect him to waltz into her room—not at all—but she knew that she would have no peace of mind unless he was physically incapable of doing so.

As it was, she didn't have much peace of mind anyway.

Her brain was buzzing with thoughts of promotion, of George—poor George—and the surprise he was going to have delivered to him the following morning in the form of Alessandro and herself, of her helplessness when it came to taking a step back from Alessandro...

She had left him sauntering towards one of the hotel lounges, where he'd intended to relax and work. She had no idea what time he had eventually returned to his bedroom, but *she* had not settled into sleep until after midnight.

Now, with her alarm buzzing her awake at seven sharp, she felt tired and unrested.

She took a few minutes just to lie there, appreciating the splendour of her surroundings. The sleeping area of her suite was twice the size of her bedroom at home. A super-king-sized four-poster bed dominated the space—wickedly, decadently romantic, with gauze curtains—and through the shimmery cream veils she could make out the sleek fitted wardrobes, the clutch of chairs by the window for relaxing...

Beyond the bedroom was an exquisite sitting area, with sofas, a concealed plasma television, a drinks cabinet...

It was a home away from home—except Kate felt anything but relaxed as she contemplated the day ahead.

Alessandro had the name of the hotel where George and his wife were holidaying. Somewhere slightly outside the main hub of the city. They would get the whole thing over and done with and then, from there, devote the remainder of the day to arranging meetings with the company he wanted to buy and two others he might or might not want to have a look at.

He had made no appointments ahead of their arrival but she knew that that would not matter. He had such clout that doors would open before he even got round to knocking on them.

'You look tense,' were his opening words as she took a seat opposite him in the dining area where they were having breakfast. He indicated the buffet area, which was extensive, and told her that a cup of strong coffee and plenty of food would settle her nerves.

'I'm not nervous,' Kate lied. 'Yes, I'm tense, because what we have to do will be unpleasant, but I'm not nervous.' Because nervousness was closely related to timidity, and they were not up sides when it came to a job promotion.

At any rate, Alessandro thought wryly, she was doing her utmost to ward off the nerves she claimed not to have by wearing yet another suit and having her hair scraped back into its habitual bun. Just in case he didn't get the message, her choice of clothes would remind him that she was here to do a job and relaxing wasn't part of the programme.

He had almost had to drag her down to have dinner with him, and even then she had kept up the professional facade that he was increasingly tempted to shatter.

The glimpses he had had of the real, living, breathing, passionate woman underneath the straitjackets she insisted on wearing 24/7 had whetted his appetite.

Of course it didn't make sense. He had enough choice in his life when it came to women not ever to make the mistake of hunting one down in his own office building. He also had enough choice to avoid any woman who gave off signals of looking for more than he was prepared to offer, and Kate Watson was definitely one of those women. He liked no-strings-attached, no-demands-made sex. She wanted strings and he was pretty sure she would be demanding. Not for her a few casual words of warning and then full steam ahead.

But he couldn't get that image of her wearing those shorts and that cropped top out of his head. He couldn't forget how she looked without make-up, with her hair swinging in a ponytail and those cute little freckles sprinkling her nose.

'I'm relieved to hear it,' he said.

Alessandro wondered whether she was aware of the challenge she was posing by wearing those unappealing suits at every opportunity. Maybe he should tell her that all items of clothing that were buttoned to the neck begged to be ripped off. Perhaps he could slip that into the conversation somewhere along the line. Her white, sensible blouse was buttoned to the neck…

'Are you insisting on taking me with you to dispatch George as some kind of test?'

Alessandro's eyebrows shot up. 'You mean to see if you pass out at the ordeal? We'll be dealing with a common criminal, Kate. I'm not asking you to visit a morgue and identify a body. But, like I said, it's important to know how to be tough when the occasion demands. I'm surprised that you're fixating on the stress of this fairly straightforward situation,' he added with silky assurance, 'when you brushed your last boyfriend aside because he wouldn't do as you wanted...'

Without giving her a chance to say anything, and with his eyes firmly pinned to her face, he summoned one of the many hovering waitresses and ordered them both a full breakfast.

'You'll need it. If we're heading up to see Wakeley's there's no guarantee that lunch is going to be on the agenda. We might have to grab something on the way. Now, you were about to explain how it is that this situation is bringing you out in a cold sweat when dispatching the potential love of your life didn't...'

'I was *not* about to explain any such thing!'

'Apologies. I had no idea that it was still such an issue for you...'

'It's not an issue for me!' Kate felt like a swimmer, desperately trying to fight against a current. Why had he ordered breakfast for her? She was fine with fruit and a croissant! Fine with removing herself from his suffocating presence on the pretext of taking her time to choose items from the buffet table.

'There's no need to explain why you'd rather

not discuss this. I was only making conversation, Kate. No need to panic.'

'I am *not panicking*,' she gritted tightly, and he threw her a kindly smile which implied that he didn't believe a word she was saying.

'And why,' she pressed on, snatching at the coffee and taking a restorative mouthful, 'do you insist on asking me loads of personal questions? Which have nothing to do with my job?'

'Like I said, I was only making conversation. If I'd known that you were still sensitive on the topic of your ex-boyfriend then I would never have gone there. Trust me.'

Kate resisted the urge to burst into manic laughter. Trust him? She would rather trust a river seething with hungry piranha.

'And as to asking you "loads of personal questions"…I like knowing a bit about the people who work for me—especially those higher up the pecking order, in positions of responsibility. Which, I'm sure, is where you will be very soon, given your talents… It helps if I know whether they're married, involved in a serious relationship, have children… That way I can tailor the needs of the job to accommodate their needs as much as is possible…'

He had never given it any such thought before, but now that he had it sort of made sense. Not that he would be playing by those rules. *Ever*. Still, never let it be said that he wasn't a man who didn't see things from every angle.

Kate allowed her ruffled feathers to be soothed. She had overreacted. Breaking up with her ex was not exactly state-secret fodder. Who cared? Did Alessandro Preda *really* give a damn whether she had called off a relationship years ago with a man who no longer featured in her life? Wasn't he telling the truth when he said that he was just making conversation? *Polite* conversation? The sort of polite conversation that was made every second of every day between people who didn't know one another all that well?

'It didn't work out,' she told him. 'Simple as that. And before you tell me that I'm a hypocrite, because I make such a big deal about the importance of taking relationship building seriously...'

'*Relationship building? What's *that*?*'

Something my mother never did, was the reply that immediately sprang to mind, but she bit it back because that would be perfect proof of just how much she had been influenced by her mother's behaviour.

In truth, looking back on her relationship with her ex-boyfriend, she could see that it had been built on hope—hope that he might be the one because they got along and because he ticked all the boxes. Like her, he had been studying accountancy. He had been reliable, feet firmly planted on the ground, a solid, dependable sort. He had been just the type of guy who *made sense*.

'It's when two people take the time to really establish the building blocks of a future together.'

'It sounds riveting. How do they do that?'

Kate lowered her eyes and remained silent.

'Please don't tell me you're going to slip back into *I couldn't possibly say because I'm just your employee* mode...'

'I *am* just your employee.'

'I'm giving you permission to speak your mind. Believe it or not...' he sat back as enough breakfast to feed a small developing country was placed in front of them '...I *do* have conversations with some of my employees that don't revolve exclusively around work...'

'I doubt you'd understand the sort of building blocks I'm talking about,' Kate told him politely. She stared at the mound of food facing her and wondered where to begin. She speared some egg and then eyed the tempting waffles at the side. 'Considering you're not into building relationships.'

'Fill me in. I want to see what I've been missing.'

Kate looked at him with exasperation. The man was utterly impossible, even though the smile on his face was so charming that it would knock any woman for six. She hurriedly focused on her food as her heart picked up speed and started relaying all those taboo messages from her brain to her body.

'I know you don't mean a word of that,' she retorted, glaring. 'But if you're really interested then I'll tell you. Relationship building is taking time to get to know someone else—to find out all you can about them, to open up so that they can find out all about you, and to plan a future together based on love and friendship and respect.'

'You're not selling it.'

'I'm not interested in whether I'm *selling it* or not,' Kate snapped. 'And I wouldn't expect to *sell it* to *you*, anyway!'

'So, having spent time on this relationship building exercise, at what point did you discover that the fun element was missing…?'

'He was lots of fun.'

He hadn't been. He had been nice and he had been steady, and he had been all those things she had thought she wanted, but when it had come to the crunch he had also been ultra-traditional. So traditional that he had wanted her to be the little lady whose career was secondary to his, who did as he asked, who dropped everything because he came first…

She felt a wave of self-pity as she realized that she would probably never find anyone. She would end up with a terrific career but next to no friends—and certainly no significant other doing the barbecue thing in the back garden.

And she would never know what it was like to *have fun* because she had always been adamant that having fun wasn't important—so adamant that the only important thing in life was being in control and never letting herself get swept away by emotion as her mother had.

But right now, in the depths of Cornwall, and despite her chequered past with men and jobs, Shirley 'Lilac' Watson was pretty contented.

Kate abruptly closed her knife and fork and fought against the sudden confusion rolling over her like fog.

'It just didn't work,' she said flatly. 'The time wasn't right. But that doesn't mean I didn't put my heart and soul into it. And that's all I have to say on the subject—I don't want to discuss it again. It's not relevant. And it's not always just about *fun*.'

This to try and stifle some of the sudden misgivings that had swept over her—dark thoughts that some of the choices she had made in her life might not have been the right ones, even if they had been made with all the right intentions.

'You're probably right.'

But she barely heard him. His soothing agreement floated around her and dissipated.

'I know for…for some people…' she only just

managed not to pin *him* as one of those people
she was talking about '…*fun* is all about *sex*, but
as far as I'm concerned there's a great deal more
to relationships than sex…'

She glared at him defiantly, challenging him to
argue with her, but Alessandro had no intention
of doing any such thing.

He had never registered much interest in ana-
lyzing women, or trying to plumb their hidden
depths, but in this instance he could see the pat-
tern of her life as clearly as if it had been printed
in bright neon letters across her forehead.

She had instilled such a strict code for herself
that she was a prisoner of it. He doubted she had
ever had any sort of fun with that ex-boyfriend of
hers, and he wondered what fun she had now, with
her stable job and her bright future. Her head told
her what she needed, but what she needed was not
necessarily what she *wanted*.

And he got the impression that she was thinking about that conundrum for the first time in
her life.

Because *he* had rammed it down her throat.

On the one hand he had done her a favour. She
was so uptight that she would snap in two given
a slight breeze. Life was not kind to the seriously
uptight. He was certain of that. They were always
the ones who ended their lives thinking about all
the things they'd strenuously resisted doing.

On the other hand she was visibly upset—and that was hardly a positive way for a boss to encourage his employee to start the day.

'You haven't finished your breakfast,' he told her, indicating her plate.

She smiled, thankful for the change in conversation and the reprieve from her thoughts.

'I don't think I've ever sat in front of a bigger breakfast.'

'Bigger is better—that's the motto, I think. We can stick to the buffet tomorrow.'

'I didn't have much appetite anyway,' Kate admitted. 'I guess I really *am* nervous about what today's going to bring. Normally I eat like a horse. Perhaps we should think about going.' She dug into her capacious handbag and extracted her tablet. 'I've brought along all the information I have on George, in case you want to sit down with him and go through it.'

Alessandro had no intention of doing any such thing, but he was relieved that she was back to normal—back to her usual efficient self, back to being the woman who matched the uniform of suits she always wore.

Even though those moments just then, when he had seen her vulnerability, had merged into the other moments when he had glimpsed the woman underneath the navy suits…strangely alluring, weirdly appealing…

Impatient with himself, he signalled a waiter in order to sign for the breakfast and flung his linen napkin next to his plate. 'Right.' He stood as he signed the bill. 'Let's get going.'

It was as though their very personal conversation had never happened. He was all business. Even without the business suit.

'Shall we get a taxi there? Do you know whether it's a long drive out of the city centre?'

'We won't need a taxi.' He flicked his cell phone out of his pocket and scrolled though the numbers. 'I've arranged to have my own driver for the duration of our stay here. More reliable and more convenient than trying to find a taxi when we need one.'

'The limo…?'

'No.'

They began strolling out to the street and she followed him as he expertly made his way through the grand hotel and the designer shopping centre that circled it.

He looked at her, his eyes creased with amusement. 'I didn't think that my conscience could stand the guilt caused by the carbon footprint.'

There he went again, she thought with a little flurry of desperation. Undoing all her plans to ignore him by being…*funny*. By saying something that made her want to smile, even though half an hour before she had been mentally snarling at him for invading her private life and asking personal questions.

He was also in business mode. She could sense that as they settled into the back of the car—a far more modest affair than the limo, though still sleek and impressive by most people's standards.

The hotel was forty minutes' drive away, which made it quite a distance out of the hub of downtown Toronto, and he turned to her and said, with a thoughtful frown, 'Seems a little odd to head for a hotel in the hills when you're spending vast sums of money on a city holiday—wouldn't you agree?'

Kate gave that some thought and nodded. 'Although some people hate cities.'

'Then why holiday in one?'

'His wife might like shopping.' She grinned. 'That's one of those building-block situations I was telling you about. He hates cities and shopping, she loves them—so they go somewhere in between.' She surprised herself by harking back to a conversation she wanted to forget, but at least it distracted her from the unpleasant task that lay ahead.

'I'm not sensing an element of compromise here…'

'Well, the next time it's her turn to give in and allow him more of what he wants.'

'For instance…?'

Kate shrugged. 'He might want to…I don't know…go fishing, rent a cottage in the Cotswolds and have long walks, head up to Scotland to appreciate the wild, stunning scenery…'

'My take is that *that* particular couple aren't suited. She wants to shop…he wants to half freeze to death in the middle of nowhere to appreciate the scenery… It'll end in tears. You wait and see…'

Kate laughed. Really laughed.

She felt all her concerns melt away and their eyes met. Her breath caught in her throat because she felt as if it was an intense moment, when something intangible had been shared. Though what, she couldn't say. A shared sense of humour? A certain way they both had of finding the same thing funny…?

'Here, it might make a little more sense. You don't have to travel too far out of the city before you come slap-bang into some remarkable scenery…'

He began giving her a potted history of the place, telling her about its geographical splendours, the thousand and one sights that made it so special.

What the hell had happened just then? he wondered. He had got caught out by a curveball—had had the oddest sensation of stepping onto quicksand, a place where he was no longer in complete control but at the mercy of reactions and responses that went against the grain, against his rigidly imposed rules.

The hotel, when they finally arrived, was a modest building, with a car park in the front, sandwiched between a fast food restaurant and a shop advertising all manner of office supplies.

Kate could see that Alessandro was taken aback at the place George and his wife had chosen to stay for their vacation, but he said nothing as they walked through the glass revolving doors and straight to the reception desk, which was manned by a bored-looking girl, twirling her hair and chatting on her mobile.

Kate wondered whether they had chosen this spot because it offered access to the city but also access to the outlying countryside…pine forests, lakes…beautiful terrain to explore. She didn't know what George and his wife did for fun, aside from family stuff with their kids and grandkids. Maybe they loved mountaineering, hiking…who knew…?

The blonde twirling her hair instantly hung up and straightened as they approached the desk.

Mr and Mrs Cape… Would she buzz through to them…? Tell Mr Cape that Alessandro Preda was in Reception and wanted to have a word with him…? Tell him that Kate Watson was there as well…?

The blonde shot Kate a covert look that simmered with envy.

'Mr and Mrs Cape aren't in.' She didn't need to consult the register for this information. 'They leave at the same time every morning. Eight sharp. I can leave a message for them and get them to contact you—or you can leave a note and I'll make sure they get it as soon as they're back.'

'Which would be at what time…?'

'This evening. Six sharp.'

'Unusual sightseeing activities that can be planned with such precision,' Alessandro said with stinging sarcasm, and he received a shocked and surprised look from the blonde in response.

'Can I ask whether you're related to George and Karen?'

Alessandro raised his eyebrows expressively. *Cosy relationship with the girl at Reception?* he thought. Bit odd… Admittedly the hotel was only the size of a bed and breakfast. For all he knew that was exactly what it was, despite its grandiose name: the Ruskin Hotel. But still…

'I'm his boss, and I'm here to see him on a business-related matter.'

'If you're his boss then I'm surprised… Didn't he mention…?'

'Mention what?' Kate asked gently, reading sudden confusion in the receptionist's blue eyes.

'They go to the hospital every day. They're

CATHY WILLIAMS   149

allowed some leeway with the visiting hours, but they tend to stay there pretty much for the whole day, so that they can be there for Gavin and Caroline.'

'Caroline's their daughter...' Kate turned to Alessandro, her mind a whirl. 'Gavin's their son-in-law. I know that because there's a family photo on his desk...'

'Right. Hospital. Perhaps you could tell us which hospital this is...?'

They arrived at the hospital in under an hour. It had been a largely silent journey. For the first time Alessandro had been caught on the back foot—handed information he had not been expecting... information that altered the straightforward situation he'd thought he would be dealing with.

Despite the fact that George and his wife had chosen to stay outside the city, the hospital was actually in downtown Toronto. Kate guessed that either the little hotel was very reasonably priced, or else they had some experience of being there before. Or maybe they just needed to be outside the main drag of a city to clear their heads at the end of the day.

A long day.

Because the days *would* be long. In the back of the car Alessandro had looked up the hospital on the internet, so they both knew that it was a centre for the treatment of sick children.

Now, as they approached the white-fronted building visible through a bank of trees, Alessandro turned to her and spoke for the first time.

'This is not what I expected,' he said roughly, raking fingers through his dark hair. 'And you won't be accompanying me into the hospital.'

'Perhaps we should wait until they're back at the hotel this evening. And I *will* be accompanying you, by the way.'

'It wasn't a suggestion, Kate. It was an order.'

'And my answer wasn't a suggestion either. It was a statement of fact.' She sighed. 'I'm very fond of George. He's been good to me, and I want him to know that I'm here for him and his wife. Whatever the outcome of your...*talk* with him.' She paused and looked at Alessandro's averted profile. His beautiful eyes were veiled.

He turned to her before opening his door. 'Stubborn.'

'Yes, I can be.' She stuck her chin out defiantly, prepared to go all the way into an argument, but there was no argument as he shrugged and stepped out of the car, waited for her to join him.

She wished she could reach into his head and see what he was thinking. She had the strangest urge to rest her hand on his forearm in a gesture of comfort, although she had no idea what she would be comforting him *for*—unless it was just for getting something wrong, for showing himself to be fallible like the rest of the human race.

She didn't imagine that he liked being wrong. She thought that he had probably never been wrong about anything in his entire life—at least not when it came to business. In business—and this *was* a business matter after all—his judgement would always have been faultless.

'Stubborn can sometimes be a good thing,' he mused, glancing down at her.

'What…what do you intend to do?' she ventured, half running to keep up with him and longing for a bit of cool, because she was beginning to overheat in her outfit.

'I intend to play it by ear…'

'Can *that* sometimes be a good thing?'

'I'll let you know later. Can't say it's something I've ever done before.'

They entered the cool foyer of the hospital, and after that everything seemed to happen very quickly.

Alessandro commanded attention. How did that work when he wasn't Canadian, wasn't a doctor and had no connections to the hospital? It just did.

Within half an hour they knew where they could locate George, and after an hour and a half—during which time they sat in a very modern, very nice restaurant in front of cups of coffee, with Alessandro working via his smartphone and Kate pretending to be hard at it in front of her tablet—George came to meet them.

A wearily resigned George, who had obviously sussed why they had landed up in Toronto and at the hospital.

Kate's heart went out to the older man. He was in one of his usual trademark brightly coloured outfits. She had always smiled at that. Even when he was in a suit his shirt was always jolly, his tie was always patterned, his hankies were always ridiculously gimmicky. He had told her once, laughing, that his wife chose his shirts, his daughter chose his handkerchiefs and his grandchildren chose his socks. So what chance did he ever have of looking debonair?

He seemed to have shrunk—or maybe she was only noticing that now because he looked so weary.

'I know why you've come,' were his opening words as he sat opposite them with a cup of coffee. He looked at Alessandro with resignation. 'Of course I was going to be found out. I'd hoped that somehow I would have managed to start repaying what I... I want to say what I *borrowed*, but I realize, Mr Preda, that you probably won't see it that way...'

'You have no idea how I'm going to see it, George. So why don't you start from the beginning and leave nothing out...?'

* * *

It was after six by the time their day was done. And every second of it had been spent at a high-voltage pace that had left Kate breathless, barely able to keep up.

Now, as she tripped along in Alessandro's wake, she ran her fingers through her hair, which had unravelled, been scooped back up again, and then unravelled again—so heaven only knew what she looked like now. Not the consummate professional, she was betting.

'Alessandro…' she breathed, only realizing afterwards that it was the first time she had addressed him by his Christian name without feeling awkward.

Alessandro stopped en route to his very patient driver, who had been on call throughout the day and was probably as exhausted as she was.

He shot her an expressive and very wry look. 'Well? Get it over and done with…'

'What?'

'A tender-hearted comment about my soft side… Have I turned into one of those, caring, sharing touchy-feely types who do foot massages for their loved ones every evening before running them a hot bath and cooking them a slap-up meal?'

'I *have* seen a different side to you…'

'Same side as always,' Alessandro told her

drily. 'You're just choosing to interpret it in a different way. There would have been no point prosecuting George.'

'You did more than just not prosecute him,' she pointed out.

But she wasn't going to run away with a long explanation of exactly what had transpired over the past few hours. He might tell her that he had been as tough in his dealings as he always was, but he hadn't.

George's granddaughter was ill. Tears had sprung to his eyes as he had described the speed of little Imogen's disease and their dismay when they had discovered that the prognosis in the UK was not favourable.

They had scoured the internet—searching for hope, really—and it had come in the form of a revolutionary breakthrough treatment in Toronto. But it was treatment that came at a price, and hence his dipping into money that didn't belong to him. Because he had already used all his savings— every scrap of money that had been put aside for his retirement—on the initial consultations and the first lot of treatment.

Alessandro could have listened and stuck to the programme: *You ripped me off and you're out— save your excuses for the judge.*

Even at her most optimistic she'd thought he might have acquitted George of blame, understood the extenuating circumstances and been sympathetic when it came to a repayment scheme.

Instead, he had not only heard the older man out and absolved him of having to repay the debt, but he had taken charge of everything. He had dealt with the bank, set up an account for George's daughter, then spoken to the hospital, assured them that the treatment would be covered whatever the cost. He had also—and this had made her heart constrict—informed George that he would not have to see out his old age in penury.

Alessandro Preda, a hard man in the world of finance, a guy who was ruthless in his business dealings, had gone beyond the bounds of duty.

'True,' he agreed, stepping aside so that she could precede him into the car. 'And of course he should have spoken to me before he did what he did…' He sprawled back against the door, facing her, his handsome, lean face amused and speculative.

'But all's well that ends well…' Kate inserted hurriedly. 'Although we didn't get to visit your client. Will that be on the agenda for tomorrow?'

'Tell me you're *not* about to stick on your business hat after the day we've had?'

Kate licked her lips, nervously aware of his eyes fastened to her face. She had completely forgotten throughout the course of the day that she had to be careful when she was around him. She had seen another side to him and had been swept away by the revelation.

Which didn't change the fact that she still heartily disapproved of him on a number of fronts…

'Because I'm too tired to start thinking about cutting deals…'

'Of course.'

'And I'm surprised you don't feel the same.'

'I suppose I could do with a little downtime…'

'Splendid. Because tonight we'll go out for dinner, do a little city exploring. We can both knock business on the head for a couple of hours— wouldn't you agree?'

'Dinner…? City exploring…?' she asked, dry-mouthed.

'Or you can call it "downtime". Whatever you prefer. And you're *not* going to be wearing a suit.'

'But that's pretty much all I—'

'Then use the company account to buy something more suitable to wear. You *have* got a company account, haven't you?'

'Yes, but—'

'Then it's settled. Today has been a day full of surprises,' he murmured, in a soft voice that was as devastating to her senses as a caress. 'I've surprised you. Now it's your turn to surprise me… Be someone more than just the prim and proper busy little bee. Do you think you can do that? Or is it too much of an ask…?'

CHAPTER SEVEN

"IS IT TOO much of an ask?"

If he had just insisted on dinner, ignored her protests, basically commanded her to relax in his company, then reluctantly she would have agreed, because she would have had no choice. And she would have donned one of her various suits because it was vitally important to maintain the boundary lines between them.

Boundary lines that, yet again, were in danger of being breached.

But that amused, mocking, *"Is it too much of an ask?"* question had got her back up.

How buttoned up did he think she was? Did he imagine that she was incapable of ever letting her hair down? Did he think that she was such a dull Miss Prim and Proper, glued to her tablet, that she quailed at the prospect of shedding her work clothes and taking time out to be a normal young woman?

Or maybe he thought that she just quailed when the shedding of her work clothes threatened to take place *in his company.* The man might have shown her a side that was curiously empathetic in his dealings with George, but that didn't mean he wasn't still the arrogant guy who took what he wanted from women and chucked them out when he decided the time had come to move on.

But if he insisted that she go shopping—that she use the company account to buy stuff she probably would never wear again—then why not?

Toronto was full of wonderful shops. Shops that lined the streets or were packed into malls.

It was still so hot outside that she opted for the Eaton Centre. She had no idea what she intended buying. It wouldn't take long. She loathed shopping. It was just one of those things that needed doing now and again, under duress.

Her mother had been a shopper. Kate could remember being dragged from shop to shop, spending money they could ill afford on garish outfits. By the age of eleven she had grown accustomed to sitting outside changing rooms, her head firmly planted in a book, while her mother tried on clothes. It had been toe-curlingly embarrassing. She had so desperately wanted her mother just to...*to look like all the other mothers.* How hard would that have been? Plain trousers? Tops that didn't cling or have plunging necklines? Shoes that didn't have five-inch heels and were never, *ever* worn with tight white jeans?

How hard would it have been for her just to *avoid wearing bright red*?

Her mother had never complained at the little digs she had thoughtlessly inflicted over the years. The not-so-gentle hints that maybe she should *tone it down*. She had laughed and told her to loosen up a little—had tried to get her out of her jeans and baggy jumpers into the occasional dress. Shirley Watson might not have been good when it came to all the stuff Kate had considered crucially important, she might have failed to take the appropriate level of interest in parents' evenings and homework projects, but she had never tired of trying to dress her up.

Kate had resisted all those efforts, and had continued doing so even when her mother had no longer been around, trying to steer her in a different direction from the one she wanted.

So now here she was.

And as she browsed through the shops she saw herself through her mother's eyes. Always a little drab. Never making anything of what she had been given.

Those were Alessandro's eyes also.

A streak of rebellion coursed through her, and as she shopped she was guiltily aware that she was enjoying shopping for maybe the first time in her life.

She wasn't buying clothes to project the image

she wanted the world to see. She was buying clothes because she liked the way they looked on her. Two dresses, a skirt that reached to mid-thigh, tops that had no buttons…and shoes that had heels and weren't black.

Though she still avoided red.

She had no idea where they would be going after the 'city exploring' Alessandro had suggested, but she didn't care.

She took her time soaking in the bath, washed her hair and *left it loose*, so that it tumbled down her back in a cascade of waves, and wore one of the dresses she had bought—a sleek, pale coral affair that did a little clinging. And she wore the high sandals she had bought too.

As she stared at her reflection in the mirror she could feel her heart beating wildly. Because this was not the Kate Watson she had spent her life cultivating.

This was a young woman who *had a life*—and an exciting one.

'Okay…' She grinned sheepishly at the stranger in the mirror. 'So we both know that that's a bit of an exaggeration—but what's the harm in having a life for one evening? Dispelling the ideas Alessandro has about me? Mum, if you could see me now, you'd be proud.'

On the spur of the moment she took a selfie and sent it to her mother, and minutes later, as she headed down to meet Alessandro in the bar, she smiled at the response she got—which was a series of exclamation marks and smiley faces.

They had arranged to meet in one of the trendier bars in the hotel and it took her a few minutes to locate Alessandro, who was sitting at the back, shielded from view by the crowds of young people milling around.

Some of those young people were turning to *look at her*. Kate was conscious of that out of the corner of her eye, and it gave her a heady little thrill as she took some time to look at Alessandro...

He glanced up and there she was. For a few seconds Alessandro's mind went completely blank. He had thrown down a challenge to her—*dress like a woman and not like a robot*—but he had doubted she would pick up the gauntlet. He had fully expected to see her in yet another tiresome version of 'The Suit', complete with discreet blouse buttoned all the way up, just in case a glimpse of her neck made her feel like a tart.

Not for a single passing second had he expected...

A vision.

He had seen her in a pair of shorts and a cropped top, but not even that had prepared him for just how beautiful she was when she stripped off the suit of armour.

She was tall anyway, but her heels escalated her to nearly six foot. Her long brown hair, streaked with shades of chestnut and deep gold, flowed down her back and over her narrow shoulders, and the dress, in some peachy colour that would have made most women look washed out, was glorious against her skin tone.

Glorious, and clinging in all the right places.

A surge of purely masculine appreciation kicked in with force. He watched as she glanced through the crowded bar, noticed as eyes were turned in her direction, realized that he wasn't the only one in the room feeling a surge of purely masculine appreciation.

He relaxed back, half smiling as she sashayed towards him.

Who would have guessed that she could *sashay*? But then prissy, starchy suits weren't conducive to sashaying, were they? Neither were sensible flat black pumps...

But a peach-coloured dress that lovingly cupped generous breasts, clung to a slender waist and fell to mid-thigh with a frilly little kick was definitely the stuff that sashays were made of...

He wondered whether it would be politically incorrect to insist in the contract for her promotion that she only wear clothes conducive to sashaying...

'I see you went shopping...' he said, rising to

his feet as she approached him. In heels, she was almost at his eye level. Eye make-up. A charcoal colour on her lids that gave her a sultry, sexy look. And just a shimmer of lip gloss, emphasizing the fullness of her lips.

An inconvenient erection was making itself felt, pushing against his zipper.

'You were right.' Kate sat down hurriedly. Because, unusual and satisfying as it was to garner stares from other people, her prurient streak was just a little too insistent to ignore for very long. 'My suits are way too formal and hot for the weather over here, so I've invested in one or two things...'

She discreetly tugged at the hem of the dress, which had ridden up and was exposing too much thigh for her liking.

'Very wise,' Alessandro murmured gravely. 'Although you might have gone to the other extreme. If you plan on wearing sexy little numbers like this during the day...it might be a little too dressy...'

Kate's breathing hitched and her eyes widened at the slow, lazy smile that lightened his features.

'This is just a normal...er...dress,' she stammered, mesmerized by the gleam in his eyes. 'Nothing that any other woman in here isn't wearing.'

Alessandro made a show of looking around him

before resting his dark eyes on her flushed face. 'But not many of them have the body to pull it off. You must know that.'

'I...'

'I admit I was a little surprised when I saw that you had taken me at my word. Aside from the time when I surprised you in your house, I honestly thought that your entire repertoire of clothes was comprised of suits in various shades of grey and navy...'

'I don't have much use for... I don't usually...'

'Paint the town red in snappy little numbers that attract attention?'

So what had she expected? That they would talk about work? When he had specifically told her that work was the last thing he wanted to think about after the day they had had with George and his sad, disturbing revelations?

'I've never been one for going to clubs.' She couldn't conceal a shudder. 'So, no, this is the one and only dress I have along these lines. Well, aside from the other one I bought today. Now I have two.'

'Two? I don't know why, but that strikes me as a little sad...' He grinned, and she blushed and looked away.

'You're winding me up again, aren't you?'

'More stating a fact,' Alessandro told her drily.

'Maybe we should play truant tomorrow and go shopping again...'

'Haven't you made arrangements for us to visit the company that you're interested in buying? I heard you on the phone when we were driving back from the hospital...'

'Arrangements are made to be broken. The company isn't going anywhere, and besides...' he shrugged carelessly '...they're keen to sell and they won't find a better buyer than me.'

'Well, thanks for the offer, but I'm all shopped out. It's not something I do unless I have to, and—'

'You really need to start living your own life, Kate, instead of the one prescribed by your mother's lifestyle.'

He poured her a glass of wine from the bottle that was chilling in a cooler on the table. 'Your mother liked shopping for clothes you deemed inappropriate, so your instant reaction was to dislike shopping and to dress in clothes your mother probably wouldn't be seen dead in.'

Kate gulped down some wine and glared at him. 'I'm getting paid to work while we're over here,' she pointed out.

He smiled at her. 'And I'm telling you that you're off the hook tomorrow. If you don't tell, then I won't.'

'You *like* shopping? With a *woman*?'

'In answer to question number one—can't stand

it. I have someone who knows the sort of clothes I wear. I leave it to her to stock my wardrobe.'

'Who? Who *does* that?'

'Let's just say that a long time ago I went out with a woman who got a little more involved than she should have…'

'You mean she wanted more than just a one-night stand?'

Kate couldn't believe she had actually said that to Alessandro, but this whole expedition was beginning to take on a slightly surreal air—and, frankly, if he wanted to command her to relax, then he would just have to take the consequences. The thrill of being *daring* and *reckless*, of releasing some of her tightly wound strings, soared through her veins, making her giddy.

'I don't do one-night stands,' Alessandro informed her.

Kate laughed aloud.

'Where's the joke in that? I'm missing it.'

'I thought…I thought you were a guy who didn't do long-term relationships?'

'The opposite of *long-term* isn't *one-night stand*. There's a very happy middle ground—trust me. Now, drink up and let's go out. I've asked the concierge for a couple of recommendations and he's booked a restaurant for us within walking distance.' He eyed her shoes. 'Are you going to be mobile in those?'

Kate stuck out her foot and inspected it, turning it round in a circle. The shoes were wonderful. The first pair of high, strappy sandals she had ever owned.

'Yes, you have a lovely foot,' Alessandro told her. 'Nice toes. Very good ankle. Would you like to twirl the other one for my inspection?'

'I wasn't fishing for compliments.'

'Of course you were. Woman's prerogative.'

'They're a little tricky to walk in…'

'We'll take it slowly—and if you feel yourself toppling over, don't worry. I'll catch you.'

Kate's head filled with that thought. It was as if someone had switched on a lightbulb, illuminating dark corners and lots of murky thoughts she had been shying away from.

Alessandro Preda might represent everything she disdained, but he was sexy and he was charming—was it any wonder that she was attracted to him? Against all odds? For so many reasons it was all wrong. She worked for him. He was a player. He was way too good-looking, too rich and too self-assured for his own good. And, yes, she was inexperienced.

All those things combined into a heady mix—which was why, as they left the bar, she could feel a powerful thread of excitement racing through her veins, so that she was hyper-aware of him next to her, practically brushing her arm with his.

The restaurant was much further from the hotel than she had thought, and she could feel the steady burn of developing blisters as they navigated the crowds, but there was no way she was going to mention that to him. Besides, what could he do?

She sighed with relief as they entered the blessed cool of a fish restaurant and discreetly kicked off the sandals underneath the table as they sat down.

The backs of her feet stung and her toes were throbbing. Thank God he had begun to talk to her about the electronics company he wanted to take over, because she could plaster an interested look on her face and focus on that instead of trying to subdue the pain.

'And so,' Alessandro concluded, 'the entire company was sucked into a black hole, to disappear into the ether...'

'Absolutely!' Kate chirped, tentatively feeling one blister with her toe and trying hard not to wince. 'It's *such* a good idea and I'm sure it'll all work out. I'll make sure to look up the company and do some research...er...later tonight...'

'I've never been able to resist a woman who hangs onto my every word,' he drawled. 'Have you heard a word I've been saying for the last ten minutes?'

'You were talking about the electronics company...'

'Care to recap? Ah. Thought not. Tell me I'm not such a bore that you lost interest in my conversation after five seconds…?'

'I'm sorry. I was miles away.'

'Anywhere in particular?'

Yes, in a world of pain and agony where my only mission was to get hold of some blister plasters and paracetamol.

'Nope. Just…just thinking about being here in North America… You know, I've done next to no travelling? I guess I was just overwhelmed by all the sights and sounds. I got lost filtering them all in my…'

Wine had been brought to them. When had that happened? She gulped down most of her glass in the hope of discovering some restorative or anaesthetic qualities to help her get through the evening without making a complete fool of herself.

'You must have been abroad, though, at some point in your life…?'

'Ibiza.' She rolled her eyes and grimaced. 'I took my mum.'

'And?'

'And it was…fun—although Mum did spend quite a bit of time flirting with the waiters.' Kate laughed. 'But, thinking about it, it really *was* fun. She made me put away every single textbook I had taken with me—I had been studying for exams—and she forced me to repeat that I was there to *relax* whenever I mentioned tax laws, or corporate finance laws, or profit and loss columns or dividends. She also made me wear my swimsuit *without* a great big tee shirt over it—even though I told her all about the dangers of too much sun and overexposure.' She sighed and looked at him. 'You must think me the last word in dull…'

'Not dull, no. Just a little…cautious…'

'And I guess you've never been cautious?'

'None of us is exempt from being careful when it comes to certain situations,' Alessandro murmured. 'Now, choose whatever you want from the menu—and don't be afraid to eat to your heart's content. The concierge tells me that the chocolate brownie pudding on the menu is famous…'

Lots of very good food, far too much very good wine and Alessandro Preda as a dinner companion—it all went a long way to numbing the pain in her feet, and she only woke up to the reality that her blisters were still there, alive and kicking, as she wriggled her feet into the sandals at the end of the meal.

The walk was less than half an hour, the air was still warm and they weren't jogging at speed—but every step was agony and it was only when the hotel was in sight that she heard herself give a soft moan, partly out of relief that her ordeal would soon be over, partly because she just couldn't help herself.

'What?' she asked brightly when he stopped and looked at her narrowly.

'What's wrong?'

'Nothing. Just taking it easy…enjoying the buzz… It's very different from London, isn't it? Not as hectic.'

Alessandro cocked his head to one side, then took his time looking at her, those clever dark eyes travelling the length of her body until they rested on her feet.

'Hell!' He stooped to examine her feet and she uttered a little shriek of mortification.

'Get up!' she whispered. 'Please, Alessandro! People are looking at us! They're going to think… to think that you're *proposing* or something!'

'To your feet?' He glanced up at her and she kept her face firmly averted. 'How long have you been in pain?'

'I'm not *in pain*. My feet might be a bit sore because I'm not used to wearing heels. Or sandals…'

'Good God, woman.'

He vaulted upright and then scooped her up in one fluid, easy movement. She squealed and clutched him, shocked rigid as he began striding towards the hotel while people turned to stare and laugh.

'Put me down!' she wailed. 'Everyone's staring!'

'You worry too much about what other people

think. And I'm not putting you down. I'm only just about hanging on to my temper. Why the *hell* didn't you say something earlier?'

'They were fine at the restaurant!'

It was hard to talk whilst trying to wriggle into some sort of position that wasn't utterly humiliating. Was her underwear on display for everyone to have a look at? She wriggled frantically, ignoring his commands to keep still, hating him at that moment in time even if he *had* rescued her from having to hobble for the rest of the way.

'*Please* put me down when we get into the hotel. I can manage from there.'

He ignored her and headed straight for the reception desk. In her head she could picture the curved marble counter, manned by banks of cruel, sniggering young girls, as she heard him ask for a comprehensive first-aid kit to be sent to his suite immediately. No, a doctor wouldn't be required—just get the kit up to his quarters double quick.

She gave up protesting and clung to him, arms around his neck, fingers clasped, eyes squeezed tightly shut—because that way she could kid herself that none of this was happening.

She only opened her eyes when she was gently lowered onto his bed, and then she watched as he even more gently removed the offending sandals and cursed softly under his breath.

'You've probably done your back in,' was all she could find to say.

'My back is fine—which is more than I can say for your feet. They're raw.'

'I'm not used to wearing heels. Or shoes like this.'

Embarrassment washed over her as he rested her aching, swollen feet on his lap and reached for the first-aid kit, which had already been placed on the bed.

'You're right. I should have mentioned earlier that I was developing one or two blisters... But, please, I can take care of this myself.' It was a last desperate plea that she thought he might ignore—and he did.

His hands were so soothing... Kate closed her eyes and her breathing slowed as he dealt with her blisters, gently cleaning them, putting cool cream on them, and then the special plasters from the kit. Maybe blisters were a common occurrence here? she thought drowsily. Maybe every silly tourist took to the streets in inadequate footwear and returned to the hotel in need of a first-aid kit?

'I had no idea that you were a doctor along with everything else,' she murmured, joking because the silence was so intense and somehow so *intimate.*

'I had planned on doing medicine, as a matter of fact...'

Her eyes flickered open. She looked at his dark head, bent down, those long brown fingers working quickly and efficiently on sorting out her feet. 'Really?'

'Really,' Alessandro said drily, without glancing in her direction. 'It was a short-lived ambition.'

'Why?'

This time he did look at her. Briefly. Dark eyes serious. 'My feckless parents needed me to set them on the financial straight and narrow.'

Now why had he said that? When he never confided in anyone—least of all a woman? When he knew that confidences encouraged women to think that they could inch their way beyond his barriers...when he knew that a woman in possession of a confidence was a woman who felt she had the upper hand...

But it had been an unsettling day. He had had his preconceived notions smashed, had been forced to re-examine the black-and-white approach to life that had always stood him in good stead. Things were always so much clearer without grey areas. And now this... His body messing with his head in a way it had never done before, controlling him as he sat here with her feet on his thigh...

'What do you mean?' Kate asked curiously. 'I thought...'

'That I was born with a silver spoon in my mouth?'

'More golden,' she admitted haltingly.

'In a way you'd be right,' he said thoughtfully, drawing back to look at his handiwork with satisfaction. 'I *am* the product of two wealthy families. My parents had more money than they knew what to do with. Unfortunately neither of them possessed the common sense to manage their fortunes properly.'

He smiled wryly and stood up, flexing his muscles, packing away the first-aid kit and then strolling to the window, where he stood for a few seconds gazing down at the street below before turning to her.

'That's love for you,' he said, and walked slowly back towards the bed, then stood at the side, hands shoved into his pockets, his lean, handsome features hard. 'The soulmates, let's-put-together-the-relationship-building-blocks kind of love you find so seductive...'

'What do you mean?' She looked at him in confusion.

'I mean...' He smiled with cool introspection. 'I have first-hand experience of how a couple of soulmates can encourage each other into lifestyles that are self-obsessed and destructive. My parents married young, and by the time they hit forty they'd managed to squander most of their joint inheritances on…well, frankly, on crap investments and eco-nonsense schemes. They lived with their heads in the clouds. Yes, they were in love—but, personally, I think if there had been a little less love and a little more common sense they might have not spent their lives hurtling from one ridiculous investment to another. Until, of course, it was up to me to bail the pair of them out.'

'*You* had to bail them out?'

'They misguidedly thought that the well would never run dry.'

'So you gave up your dreams of being a doctor for a…a more profitable lifestyle…?'

'Don't get carried away, Kate. Being in my position is hardly a hardship.'

'No…but money doesn't really matter, does it?'

'Is that why you spend every second being a businesswoman in an attempt to advance your career and get financially stable? What did I tell you about hypocrisy…? Tut-tut…'

Kate reddened. Standing over her, he was so damned tall, overwhelming her with his physicality. Her mouth dried. She couldn't tear her fascinated gaze away from him. She was suddenly conscious of her bare legs, the small dress, of the heat racing through her body inflaming her pulse, tightening the buds of her nipples into hard, pointed peaks.

'Now, here's the strategic difference between us,' Alessandro drawled softly.

She had propped herself up against the pillows and he took his time following the long, slender lines of her body before leaning down, palms flat on the bed, so that his face was only inches away from hers.

'*I* haven't abandoned having fun in favour of some never-never dream of perfection that won't be happening.'

'I haven't done that!'

'No? So when was the last time you had sex?'

Just like that the room shrank to the size of a cardboard box and breathing became difficult. Her heart was beating so hard that she could almost hear it. When she opened her mouth the professional woman with an agenda not to be affected by him had vanished. In her place was a woman in the grip of desire, a woman with needs—a woman who could feel those needs in the liquid moistening between her thighs, dampening her underwear.

'I… Well…'

'When was the last time you just *let go*, Kate…? Here's what I'm thinking… Tonight was probably the first time in years that you went out in something other than the sort of clothes someone's great-aunt would be proud to be seen in…'

'That's not fair,' she whispered, stung because it was true—horribly, mortifyingly *true.*

'It may not be *fair*, but it's true. When was the last time you felt anything but a need to work, so that you can avoid ending up in the same pickle your mother did? It's a dry life.'

'It's…'

'Dry, sterile… You're hiding away from emotion, waiting for the Big Thing to happen, and in the meantime life's passing you by.'

'It's not all about sex…'

He didn't answer. He didn't have to.

She could read the intent in his eyes and she knew that he was going to kiss her—*and she wanted him to.* She wanted him to with every fibre of her sex-starved being…even if it made no sense.

His mouth covered hers, and it wasn't with the possessive hunger of a man who wanted to take without giving. No, it was a slow, lazy, lingering kiss…a melding of tongues that had her whimpering. She linked her fingers behind his neck and drew him to her—only to pull back and look at him with huge, bewildered eyes.

'We shouldn't be doing this,' she whispered huskily.

What a joke! She still had her hands behind his head and her body was still leaning towards his.

Tell me about it, Alessandro thought. This was

probably the *last* thing he should be doing. But for the first time in his life his control had slipped and he had no intention of trying to claw it back. He was so turned on that he could barely think clearly. He wanted to feel her hand on his erection, feel her rubbing him, licking him, taking him into her mouth…

Instead they were both still fully clothed, and it was driving him crazy.

'It's better to do the things we know we shouldn't do than live an empty life resisting all temptation,' he husked. 'But if you want me to stop…'

'I don't even approve of you…'

'I know.'

He silenced her with another kiss, and this time it was hungry, urgent, demanding and utterly, utterly devastating.

She was barely aware of him getting onto the bed with her, or of him rearing up to strip off his shirt. She was too fascinated by the sight of his bare torso…bronzed, broad-shouldered, every ripple of muscle defined.

She moaned and levered herself up, licked his stomach. It felt so decadent and so wanton that she could scarcely believe she'd done it. He flung back his head and she felt him suck in his breath. Lord, but that made her feel powerful.

Tentatively, she placed her hand on the bulge

pushing against his trousers, and was thrilled when she heard him groan and felt him press her hand down hard.

'Just...wait...' Alessandro held his breath, gathering his scattered self-control, then released it in a long, slow hiss.

'Wait for what?'

'I...have never...been so close to doing the unthinkable...'

'What's that?'

Alessandro looked down at her flushed face and grinned with wicked enjoyment. 'Coming before I want to—shall I show you what it feels like?'

His dark eyes were bold as they raked over her. She had no idea how he could do this, but she knew that he had done it before—looked at her and made her feel as though she was being touched, caressed.

So it was a bad idea. It didn't make sense. It went against every principle she had ever held. Sex was not something to be given away lightly—it should be part of a developing relationship, a journey of discovery and exploration.

Alessandro Preda had about as much interest in journeys of discovery and exploration as a pirate sizing up his next conquest. *See, take and move on* was not the motto of the sensitive kind of guy she needed.

But, God, she wanted him. And wasn't he right?

She had been so busy building her secure little nest that she had forgotten there was a world out there—a world of experience and fun and adventure and...*challenge*.

Why shouldn't she accept the challenge and go with the flow for the first time in her life?

'I work for you...'

'I think it's too late for us to throw that into the mix...'

He straddled her and reached for the button on his trousers. One hundred per cent dominant alpha male...*one hundred per cent heartbreaker*...

But she was safe. Her heart could never be broken by a man like Alessandro Preda. Men like him had broken her mother's heart time and again. Men like him led women on, led them astray, made them forget reason. Her lifetime's work had been to make sure that she was emotionally immune to men like him. So what if it turned out in this instance that she wasn't *physically* immune? She could deal with that...

This was living in the moment. It was something she had never done. And she was going to do it now because he was right. Regret would always make a bitter companion.

CHAPTER EIGHT

THE LITTLE SILKY nothing of a dress had ridden up her thighs as she lay sprawled on the bed, watching him with bated breath.

Still straddling her, not taking his eyes off her heated face, he reached behind him without looking and cupped her between her legs.

She was melting. When he moved his hand, pressing down, she moaned and her eyelids fluttered. She was wet…so wet. She let her legs go limp, inviting him, and he took advantage of the invitation to slip his hand under her damp panties so that he could rub two fingers gently, insistently, finding the throbbing nub of her clitoris and making her gasp with pleasure.

'You like what I'm doing to you?' he murmured.

She nodded, dazed, hardly able to believe that this was *her*—sensible, practical, ever-watchful Kate Watson, who had always planned her life right down to the very last detail, who had never allowed herself to get swept up in anything she couldn't control.

She moved against his questing fingers, groaning softly, feeling the waves of pleasure beginning to rise to a crest.

'Not like this…' she managed to croak, in a voice she didn't recognize, and he withdrew his fingers immediately, leaving her aching down there. 'Beast.' She smiled at the wicked glint in his eyes.

'I'll let you do the same to me,' Alessandro soothed. 'Sometimes it works…getting so close to the finishing line and not being able to cross it…it makes the eventual crossing so much more thrilling…'

He eased his big body off the bed and took his time removing his clothes. He found that his hands were unsteady, his pulse racing, and he was momentarily confused… Because this had never happened to him in his life before. He couldn't remember *ever* having to struggle against a desire to come before the time was right. When it came to making love he had always had the ultimate control over his body.

Not now.

Now he knew that if she touched him down there, in all the ways he wanted her to, he would ejaculate. He would have to take his time, move slowly, and whilst it wasn't his style to rush, this time rushing was exactly what he wanted to do.

This loss of control was…destabilizing. It made him feel like someone tipping over the edge as they bungee-jumped into the unknown.

Her eyes were on him, fascinated, apprehensive, weirdly shy, as he stood in front of her clad only in his boxers.

'Like what you see?'

Kate nodded, her mouth dry. *Like?* That word didn't begin to sum up what she was feeling. The man was the ultimate in physical perfection. How was that even possible for someone who spent the majority of his time on a plane, or behind a desk, or clutching a cell phone…?

'You must exercise a lot,' she ventured, and he grinned.

'I'm taking that as a compliment.'

He slipped off the boxers and she nearly fainted at the sight of his impressive arousal. Her eyes were half-closed as he slipped back onto the bed next to her.

Nerves threatened to overwhelm her. For a wild moment she wondered how she had managed to end up lying in his bed, his naked body hot and demanding against hers, her own body tingling, perspiring, aching to have the flimsy dress off her—because even the slightest bit of material felt like an iron barrier between them that *had* to be removed.

This wasn't *her*. Yet, in a way, nothing had ever felt so natural. Her heart was beating like a sledge-hammer as she curved onto her side so that they were facing one another, and she marvelled at the depth of his eyes, the shades of navy that flecked the black.

'You were telling me how impressed you are with my body…' he murmured, pushing her hair back and planting a trail of delicate kisses on her face. He *wanted* to hear her say it, which was a feeling he'd never experienced before.

'Was I?'

'I do work out, as a matter of fact.'

'When? I thought you lived at the office?'

'I work hard, but I play hard as well… I like to think that that's what makes for a balanced life.'

Kate knew what he meant by *playing hard*. It wasn't trips to the gym twice a week. It was sex. No-strings sex. With beautiful women who didn't make demands because the second a demand was made their time was up.

The operative word was *play*.

It occurred to her that his sudden attack of de-sire for her had only surfaced when he had seen her out of her work uniform—when he had seen her dressed to kill and showing off her assets. As her mother had. He had gone for the body, and how many times had she told herself that she would never be—could *never* be—attracted to any man who wasn't interested in her *for who she was*.

So much for being able to rely on her brain to tell her what to do…

She wanted this man. She couldn't think past the heat sizzling through her veins, making her feel treacherously *alive* for the first time in her life.

'Why me?' she whispered.

Alessandro drew back to look at her. Up close, she was even more stunning. Her face was dewy, satiny smooth, her lips full, her eyes the purest green he had ever seen.

But he wasn't lying in this bed, his body on fire, because of the way she looked. The world—especially *his* world—was full of stunning women. After a while they simply merged into one. No, he was here because she was…*different*.

And because she had witnessed him in a rare moment of confusion—when he had had all his preconceived notions about George Cape thrown over, when he had had to think on his feet and behave in a way that hadn't been predicted by his assumptions.

Vulnerable.

He hated the word, but there it was. She had seen him strangely vulnerable.

Had that created some sort of weird bond between them? It was a thought he didn't bother to follow through to a conclusion because it made no difference. The reality was that he was here, she was here and they were going to make love.

'These things happen,' he murmured. 'Who knows what generates physical attraction? You have skin like a peach... Stop talking. There are better ways for us to expend energy.'

He ran his hand along her thigh, under the dress, along her waist. He was almost *nervous*, and that shook him a little.

Against her, Kate could feel the hardness of his erection, massive, stirring as he touched her. She reached down and held it and had another near-fainting moment.

'I'm not...experienced...like those women you go out with. I just thought I should warn you...'

'Okay. Warning duly noted. Now, I want you to get out of that dress. It's a nice dress, but I'd rather see it on the floor...'

She hitched her hands under the hem, ready to wriggle it over her head, but he stopped her.

'Not so fast...'

'What do you mean?'

Alessandro propped himself up on one elbow and looked at her with a little half smile that did all sorts of things to her already escalating levels of heat. Spontaneous combustion might very well be on the cards.

This was lust. *This* was what women went on about when they whined that they *just couldn't help themselves*. Kate had never had any sympathy at all for women like that. As far as she was concerned there was never any *not being able to help yourself* when it came to men and sex. You could *always* help yourself. She was a prime example of that and it was called self-restraint. Easy.

Except right now, if someone had told her to walk away from the man staring at her with eyes that could start a forest fire, she wouldn't have been able to move a limb.

'Time for you to do a striptease...' He lay back on the bed, hands folded behind his head, and looked at her. 'Fair's fair, after all.'

'I've never done a striptease before in my life.'

Nor had she ever wanted to! In fact, on a scale of one to ten of activities she would have avoided at all costs, performing a striptease was off the scale completely.

Just thinking about it now brought her out in a cold sweat, and yet underneath there was a dark stirring of excitement when she imagined those dark, dark eyes focused on her, enjoying her...

Did that make her weak...like her mother? Helpless in the company of an attractive man? Unable to obey what her head was telling her? Ruled by responses over which she had no control?

No. Kate knew that with gut instinct. It didn't. But she had the scariest feeling that she was letting go of the old Kate…although she had no idea where that notion came from. Or where the old Kate was going and whether she would be returning any time soon.

'You don't have to if it makes you feel uncomfortable,' Alessandro said, in a tone of voice that made her realize he could see from the expression on her face exactly what she had been thinking.

'Why would it make me feel uncomfortable?'

'Tell me something,' he said, watching as she hovered, half-sitting, poised between climbing out of her box and hanging on in there for dear life. 'When you made love in the past, was it always in the dark?'

Kate blushed—which was an answer in itself.

He reached out and lazily stroked the side of her arm. 'Have you never wanted to see what you were doing?'

'I've slept with a guy precisely four times,' she confessed in a harried rush. 'We never… I never… I suppose if things had worked out…'

No. Even if she and Sam had *not* ended up crashing and burning, she still wouldn't have become the wanton hussy she was now capable of being. Given the right guy. Or rather the wrong guy—the utterly, utterly *wrong and inappropriate* guy. She would have still insisted on having the lights out when she got undressed, because he had not induced these crazy feelings of uncontrollable yearning in her.

She slithered off the bed and stood just where Alessandro had previously stood. His discarded clothes were right there on the floor by her feet. Very slowly, and with a lack of self-consciousness that amazed her, considering she should be ravaged by it, she drew the slip of a dress over her head and tossed it on the ground, where it joined his clothes.

Then she reached behind her and unclasped her bra.

Alessandro touched himself. His breathing faltered. She was slender, but not skinny, and her breasts were generous, barely contained within the flimsy bra. Her nipples were large, pink, begging to be sucked. Just thinking about it made the breath hitch in his throat even more.

She stepped out of her underwear and then drew herself up proudly, all woman, curves in all the right places, the downy patch between her thighs proclaiming her as one of the few who *didn't* think it necessary to depilate every square inch of her body.

Alessandro had never been so turned on in his entire life.

As if suddenly remembering that she should be quivering with embarrassment she lowered her eyes and blushed madly, before making a dive for the safety of the bed. But he stopped her in her tracks by placing one big hand on her stomach.

'Your feet still look tender,' he murmured, gazing at her plastered heels and arches.

Blistered feet should do *something* to get his raging libido a little under control—but actually, as he stared down, all he could see were her extremely shapely ankles, and all he could smell was the heady, musky perfume from between her legs.

He groaned and curved both hands to cup her bottom, tugging her gently towards him.

Kate had forgotten about the sore feet that were the reason she was in this bedroom in the first place. They were consigned to oblivion now, as she took those tentative steps into…the unknown…

'I…I can't…' She managed to articulate those strangulated words while, of their own accord, her fingers curled into his hair.

She gasped when he parted those soft folds, and gasped again as his tongue flicked against the wet, sensitized flesh, and then she stopped gasping and drew in her breath, holding it as that exploring tongue began to explore some more.

It was exquisite. She was transported to another dimension. And she parted her legs, accommodating that questing tongue as it located the throbbing nub of her swollen clitoris. She arched back. Her whole body was covered in slick perspiration. If a bomb had dropped on the hotel right now she was pretty sure she wouldn't have noticed—because the only thing she was capable of noticing was the sweep of sensations racing through her body at breakneck speed.

When he withdrew she practically sobbed with the sense of loss.

'*Now* you can come to bed,' Alessandro commanded softly.

He patted the space next to him and she slid like a rag doll into the allotted spot, her body turning and curving against his, loving the feel of the heat he was emanating.

He pushed his thigh between her legs and moved it with just the right level of pressure to ensure that she picked up where she had left off when he had removed his tongue from her.

Kate grasped his shoulders, feeling solid muscle under her fingers, and looked at him drowsily, drugged, completely in his power.

And he liked that.

He kissed her—a hungry, very thorough kiss, that made all her bones feel just a little more jellylike—and then he carried on kissing her. The slender column of her neck, her shoulder blades, working his way down until he was circling her nipple with his tongue and then taking it into his mouth and suckling on it, lazily, in no rush to go anywhere.

She had died and gone to heaven. There wasn't a single part of her entire body that wasn't buzzing with all sorts of new, wonderful, pleasurable sensations, and they only increased when his hand wandered down to her thighs, slipped between them, his fingers idly playing with her in a way that was screamingly intimate and utterly erotic.

She squirmed and felt him smile against her breast. He was enjoying himself—but he couldn't be enjoying himself half as much as she was enjoying *herself*. He did this all the time. He had a reputation that preceded him wherever he went. He was a guy who had wined, dined and bedded some of the most beautiful women in the world. This was probably routine for him.

Not that she liked the thought of that. But she hadn't been born yesterday, and even while she was losing herself in the pleasure he was bringing her she was still realistic enough to know that he was an expert at this sort of thing. An expert when it came to giving sexual pleasure.

Whereas *she* was in a whole new territory— one she had never visited before—and she was loving it.

Loving what he was doing to her.

Loving the way her body felt—as though it was waking up for the very first time.

She closed her eyes and sighed as he moved from one tingling nipple to the other.

She had always thought her breasts to be overtly sexual—had always secretly longed for little ones that didn't require the heavy-duty support of a bra—but, watching his dark head exploring them, she was enormously proud of them, of their fullness, the prominence of her dusky nipples, which he couldn't seem to get enough of.

She moved against his fingers and he thrust them a little deeper into her, arousing her yet further.

'Please...' she pleaded, and he stopped sucking her nipple to look at her.

'Please what...?'

'You know...'

'Okay, so maybe I do, but I still want to hear you say it...'

'You want me to tell you that...that I want you? Right now? That I can't hold on for much longer? That—'

'That you'd like to come into my hand but you'd much rather feel me moving inside you...thrusting hard and deep... Repeat all that after me...'

'I can't!' she gasped breathlessly, and Alessandro grinned. Because the chasm between her wet, hot body and her prurience, to which she couldn't help but carry on clinging, even if it was just a little, fascinated him.

'You can…'

She did. And just saying those things out loud was a huge turn-on.

She was aware of him leaving her for a few seconds, felt the mattress depress when he returned, and knew that he was donning protection.

She was open and ready for him when he entered her. Although it had been a while and he was big—very big. Her tight muscles relaxed, closed round his hardened sheath, took every glorious inch of him in. And when he began moving inside her it was like nothing she had ever experienced in her life before.

Her short nails dug into his back. Both their bodies were slick, sliding against one another. He reared up just as the groundswell of sensation inside her cascaded and splintered, sending her into orbit and making her cry out.

Utterly spent. That was what Kate felt as she descended from the peak to which she had been catapulted at supersonic speed. Utterly spent and very much aware that, like it or not, she had been as vulnerable to this man's sexual charisma as all those supermodels he had dated and dispatched with monotonous regularity.

Alessandro rolled off her, took a few seconds to gather himself—because the experience had

left him on a different planet. He felt amazing—
as though he had discovered the ability to walk
on water...

Where had *that* feeling come from?

He lay on his side and looked at her body.
He cupped one breast with his hand and felt its
weight.

Kate edged away and scrabbled for the duvet,
which was solidly planted underneath them.
Horses, stable doors and bolting sprang to mind.
What was the point in succumbing to a sudden attack of shyness when she had been uttering things
that made her blush only minutes previously?

That said, what on earth had she gone and
done? Shouldn't she be in the grip of remorse?
Regret? Mortification?

'My feet feel much better...' That was the pro-
saic statement that came out of her mouth—because she was too busy looking at the man she
had just had sex with to think of anything wittier
or more profound to say.

'Sex has a way of sorting out most of life's little
problems.' He toyed with a few tendrils of her hair,
tucked them behind her ear. 'Including sore feet.'

'Really? I never knew...'

'That's because you've spent all of your adult
life avoiding it.'

*And you've spent all of your adult life avoiding
commitment.*

It was something she wanted to say. She found that she wanted him to talk to her—talk to her the way she had inadvertently been persuaded into talking to him—but that was a line that could not be breached. She knew that with every gut instinct inside her. Step over that line and she would be dismissed as casually as a stranger he had happened to bump into.

She didn't want to be dismissed. Not yet. Not when she had discovered this crazy, sensual side to her that made her feel so great—as though she could walk on water. She wanted to hang on to it for just a little bit longer.

What was wrong with that? It was human nature, wasn't it? The desire to cling on to something that made you feel good?

Not that she had any intention of being clingy. She might have taken an unexpected detour with him, but in the process she hadn't steamrollered over all her principles. She was as strong as she always had been.

She swatted away the uneasy realisation she had had earlier that she had fallen for his charm, succumbed to his animal magnetism, trodden the same mesmerized, idiotic path that those women he dated had trodden before her.

Now that the haze of unbridled passion had dissipated she decided that she was the same person she always had been but with *added dimensions*.

And how could *that* not be a good thing? How could *that* not stand her in good stead for the future that was out there waiting for her?

Mr Right was out there—and not only would he be waiting for her with a glass of chilled wine when she had had a long day…after the chilled wine he would sweep her off her feet and carry her into the bedroom and make her feel just the way the very inappropriate Alessandro Preda was capable of making her feel.

Because now the sensual side of her had been unleashed. Her ex-boyfriend might not have been the full package, but now she knew the full package was practically round the corner.

And the relief of knowing that knocked her for six.

Only now did she realize how much she had begun to accept an inevitable future in which she found no one, remained a lonely career woman, heading up the ladder with no one at her side.

She snuggled against Alessandro and laughed when she realized that their recent bout of mind-blowing sex had done nothing to depress his very active libido.

'The reason I asked you how your feet were,' Alessandro murmured in between kisses to the side of her mouth, 'is that it's occurred to me that walking is going to be fairly difficult for you tomorrow. Possibly for the next couple of days.'

Kate stilled. In a horizontal position, with this gorgeous hunk next to her and her body already eagerly anticipating round two in the sexual stakes, her feet had been the last thing on her mind. They felt right as rain, in fact.

Now she pictured shoving them into her little black pumps, feeling the tight leather pressing against the plasters, and knew that he had a point. But she was here to work. And he was first and foremost a man who put work ahead of everything else—and that would include a romp in the hay with one of his employees.

Which was what she was. An *employee*.

'I'm sure I'll be able to walk if I get some flip-flops.' She drew back and pressed her arms in front of her, shielding her bare breasts. 'It may not be the most professional look, but as long as I don't wear closed shoes I think I'll be fine. There's no need to imagine that I won't be able to do my job.'

And there's no need to imagine that because we've slept together I'm suddenly going to become anything less than the efficient person who reports to you... No need to fear that I'll turn into one of those clingy types who don't know when the party's over.

She had a desperate urge to fill him in on how she felt—to let him know that she was still in the driving seat…to let *herself* know that she was still in the driving seat.

'That's not why I mentioned the feet,' Alessandro drawled. 'Although I'd be curious to see how flip-flops work with your navy suits…'

'I did bring a beige one. It's my summer suit.'

'Oh, the levels of daring to which you've aspired… You forget: you can get rid of the suits. I've seen you in all your non-suited glory. You can actually feel free to dress down a little now when it comes to your work attire. I mentioned the feet because if you can't walk then we might have to resign ourselves to being holed up in this suite for the next couple of days…'

'What do you mean?'

'You *know* what I mean. You can feel the chemistry between us. I can't keep my hands off you.'

All her old principles rose to the surface but she fought them down—because hadn't she *wanted* to embark on this challenge? She wasn't going to get cold feet now.

'But what about the client you wanted us to visit?'

'He won't be going anywhere. At least not for a couple of days.'

'Is that the time limit you've set on this…er… situation?'

The sexy warmth on his face evaporated just like that. She could feel him pull back and knew that he was gauging the situation—weighing up the pros of having good sex against the cons of what might prove to be an awkward situation.

She hadn't heard his warning speech about not getting wrapped up in him. Was he trying to work out how he could give it now, having had mind-blowing sex with her?

'I know what you're thinking,' she said casually, lowering her eyes and trying to stanch the sudden pain twisting inside her.

'Really? You're a mind reader?'

'I'm not a mind-reader, but I'm not stupid either. I've told you how I feel about meaningless relationships. I've told you that I've never seen the point of one-night stands and sex just for the sake of sex. So you're probably scared stiff that we've slept together and now suddenly I'll be trying to drag you down to the local jeweller's to see what the rings there look like. But you couldn't be further from the truth.'

'No?'

'No,' Kate told him firmly. 'I don't know what happened here…things went down an unexpected road…but that doesn't change the fact that you're you and I'm me. For a start, I work for you. You're my boss. And that makes this all wrong.'

'Let's get past the boss/employee situation…'

'It's all right for *you* to say that.' Kate was suddenly angry at his complete self-assurance that he was entitled to do exactly what he wanted to do, without any repercussions whatsoever. 'You can turn round and sack me if you decide I'm some kind of liability.'

'And will you be? A liability?' He hadn't even thought of her as the sort to sell some tacky kiss-and-tell story to a newspaper—not that that would turn his world on its axis. He couldn't care less what people thought of him. But the idea that she might go down the tawdry route of gold-digger, out to siphon off money after sleeping with him... well, that was a horse of a different colour.

And why *hadn't* he thought of that possibility?

Because she'd struck him as a person of integrity. Was he about to be proved wrong?

But, no. He could tell instantly from the look of distaste that crossed her face that he had insulted her.

'I had to ask,' he said with cool detachment, rolling onto his back and staring up at the ceiling with his arms behind his head.

'Of course you did.' Kate's voice dripped sarcasm. 'It's only natural after you've slept with a woman to ask her whether she's about to phone a tabloid and spill the beans about sex with billionaire Alessandro Preda. If you think that I hopped into bed with you because I fancied my chances of fleecing you for money—'

He turned to her and stared her down unsmilingly. 'When you live my life you don't take anything for granted.'

'Then you must lead a sad life.' She sighed. 'I shouldn't have said that. I'm sorry. But I don't know how to behave around you now that this has happened. Every time I say something a little too frank I remember who you are. And then I start wondering how we got into this…this mess…'

'Situations like this are only a mess if they get out of hand—and they only get out of hand if one or the other becomes too involved.'

'And that would never be *you*.' She shot him a rueful glance, because whatever mess she had found herself in she was too greedy to want to get out of it just yet.

But get out she would. And before he gave her his lecture she thought that she might give him *hers*—set his mind at ease, pave the way for a dignified retreat when this little one-week working holiday was over. Because, as sure as the sun rose and set every day of every year, there would be nothing between them when they returned to London.

'Don't worry—it won't be me either,' she added quickly.

'I know.'

'You do?'

'You're looking for a soulmate, and it's not me. What we have is a purely physical thing.'

'It's not like me to do a purely physical thing…'

'Which makes me feel sorry for you.' He coolly returned her criticism of him back to her and she blushed. 'You look very fetching when you blush,' he murmured, distracted. 'And, just as an aside, don't feel that you have to tiptoe round me as though you're walking on eggshells. When you're lying in bed naked you cease to be my employee…'

And when I'm no longer lying in bed naked…? When I'm back sitting at my desk, wearing one of my many suits…? Working on the deals you're throwing at me…?

She had got caught up in a riptide, had lost all her prized control, and there was only one sure way she could think of regaining it—because if she didn't then she would be lost. It was a terrifying prospect. If she got lost where would she be? How would she ever be able to find all the landmarks that defined her life?

'You have to promise me something,' she told him seriously.

'I dislike making promises. Especially to women.'

'Well…' She drew in a deep breath and exhaled slowly. 'You're going to make *this* promise—if you don't then I'm going to…to get dressed and hobble back to my room…'

'Is that blackmail?' Alessandro asked coldly.

'Because that's something I dislike even more than I dislike making promises.'

'No, it's not *blackmail*. Are you always so suspicious of everyone's motives? No, don't answer that. You are. You can't help yourself. I want you to promise me that when we return to London this ends. And we never talk about it. Ever again. We pretend none of it happened and I go back to being your employee and nothing more.'

Alessandro raised his eyebrows, for this was the first time in his life he was being dismissed prematurely. Actually, it was the first time in his life he was being dismissed *at all*.

He shrugged and decided that it was a promise he was more than happy to make. He would have her for a week, and by the time the week was done he would be ready to move on. Kate Watson, stunning and sexy as she might be, wasn't his type. She wanted more from a man than a passing fling, and he suspected that if they were to continue their liaison all her good intentions not to get wrapped up in someone who wasn't her soulmate would be ground down—because that was just the way it was.

'So it's a deal?'

'It's a deal, and we can shake on it—but who's to say that you won't find it impossible to stick to your side of the bargain?'

'I may have…given in…but…but…I see this as

206 AT HER BOSS'S PLEASURE

a kind of adventure. I mean, I've never allowed
myself to get carried away. I never thought I would
either. But I'm glad that I have. I suppose, in a
weird way, I should thank you...'

She looked at him with shining sincerity and
Alessandro looked back at her, amused.

She was complex. An ambitious professional
who was endearingly inexperienced, a sensible
suit-wearing employee who still blushed like a
teenager. She was scrupulously honest, and seem-
ingly unaware that scrupulous honesty was *not*
part of the game when it came to sex and seduc-
tion. She spoke her mind and ignored the potential fallout.

All told, she challenged him.

Women generally didn't.

He wondered idly whether he had just been
looking in the wrong places. He wondered
whether the time wasn't drawing near for him to
move on from hit-and-run romances with obliging but empty-headed supermodels. He was no
believer in romance, but maybe the time was
drawing near for him to test the waters for something more solid.

Kate Watson had shown him that a good brain
certainly broadened the appeal. Tie that up with
a woman who wasn't searching for love and romance, who was as down to earth as he was when
it came to relationships—a woman who could

challenge him intellectually, could see marriage as something blessedly free from the vagaries of so-called *love*—and who was to say that it couldn't work?

He had become jaded. This interlude had demonstrated that. The novelty of having someone out of his comfort zone had been telling. Hell, he could hardly think straight with her lying here next to him! He needed to move on...

'Maybe...' he pulled her towards him '...I should be the one thanking *you*...'

CHAPTER NINE

ALESSANDRO SWIVELLED HIS leather chair away from his desk towards the floor-to-ceiling windows through which, at several floors up, he had nothing more inspiring than an uninterrupted view of grey skies. In the week and a half since they had returned from Toronto the blue-sky summer had morphed into a more traditional London summer of leaden skies, intermittent drizzle and the low-level complaints of a nation who had become accustomed to going out without the backup of brollies and cardigans.

His temper should have improved by now. It hadn't. He scowled and allowed himself a few satisfying seconds of thinking that change might be on the way in the form of a very shapely, very sexy lawyer, who had been nestling in his little black book, waiting for him to get in touch after their brief meeting several months previously. At the time he had been involved with a frisky little redhead, but frisky was no longer on the agenda and the lawyer seemed a far more promising bet.

True to her word, Kate had shut the door on him the second they had taken off from the airport in Toronto.

'It's been fun,' she had informed him, with a cheerful smile.

Thoughts of the sexy, shapely lawyer vanished as he remembered his response to that.

'I'm not ready for the fun to end just yet,' he had told her in a lazy drawl, absently noting that the suit was back in place.

And he hadn't been. As far as he'd been concerned the fun had only just started—so why should it end the second they touched down at Heathrow Airport? His diet, when it came to women and sex, didn't include self-denial, and he had seen no reason why that should change.

They had had an outrageously sexy week in Toronto, only just managing to squeeze in a brief visit to his potential client. It had been enough to secure the deal, and the remainder of their time in the city had been spent exploring the tourist attractions, getting more adventurous as her feet had healed, and making love. Surprisingly, he hadn't tired of her. He had felt none of his usual irritation or mildly suffocating claustrophobia at being in a woman's company even when they hadn't been in a bed.

That being the case, why *should* they have called it a day? She hadn't been of the same opinion.

He scowled and glanced at his watch. Every time he thought about the outcome of that conversation he wanted to hit something. She hadn't only kindly, *gently*, told him that it was over, she had also carried on smiling, a little puzzled smile, as though she hadn't quite understood why he wasn't *getting it*.

His ground his teeth together in smouldering fury as he recalled that.

He'd had no idea that a little dented ego could prove so difficult to shift. Was he really *so* conceited that he couldn't handle someone wanting to quit an affair before he was ready? Especially when he knew it was something that wasn't destined for the long haul anyway?

Because it wasn't. Simple as that. Kate Watson might have stepped out of her box, to do something that had never been on her agenda, but that didn't change the fact that what she wanted in life was completely different from what *he* wanted.

She wanted a long-term, no-holds-barred relationship, and that came with all the trappings he had no time for. Getting wrapped up with someone wasn't for him. Long-term, for him, would be something far more controllable—something that didn't risk disrupting the primary focus in his life, which was his work, something that wasn't... *intrusive*.

His cell phone buzzed.

Rebecca—or Red-Hot Rebecca, as she was called in certain legal circles. Long legs. Short hair. Good-looking with a seriously high-powered brain. Once upon a time, the seriously high-powered brain would not have been in his search engine, but now—yes, it definitely worked. In fact he couldn't understand what he had seen in his previous girlfriends. He couldn't envisage dating anyone now who didn't have a brain. The long legs helped—as did the attractive short bob. And when he had bumped into her a few months ago she had left him in no doubt that she was up for some quality time together.

And she wouldn't be on the hunt for romance and fairy-tale endings. She wouldn't want to take him over. She was a career woman, on her way to becoming the youngest ever lawyer to take silk. She didn't give the impression of someone who would be ready to jack all that in for a guy—any guy.

Big plus.

He picked up the call. She was on her way over. Opera was to be followed by a slap-up meal at one of the most expensive restaurants in the city. And then...who knew? Actually, he did.

His brain skidded to an inconvenient halt and veered off in a completely different direction.

Kate. In his bed at the hotel. Her long hair spread across the pillows, her arms resting lightly on her flat stomach as he undressed. Her eyes heavy with desire, turning him on until he could barely control himself—and that had been before he had even touched her.

Kate laughing, her hair blowing around her face, in the car they had rented so that he could show her some of the wild scenery that lay just a hop and a skip out of the city. She had insisted on taking a picnic and he had concurred, even though there had been a string of more-than-decent restaurants along the way.

Kate asking him gently about his past, trying to work out why he was anti-love and all its trials and tribulations… And him talking to her, telling her things he had never shared with anyone else…

He focused on that, pushing aside every other memory that threatened to rise to the surface.

He had been so damned wrapped up in the whole mind-blowing sex thing that he had dismissed her curiosity as an inconvenience rather than what he now knew it to be.

A way in.

It enraged him that even with that evidence of boundary-crossing he still hadn't been able to get her out of his head—still found himself taking cold showers in the middle of the night.

He had made sure to stay clear of her ever since they had returned to London. She was back in the bowels of the office, several floors down, busy as a little bee, he presumed. Her promotion was now general knowledge, as was George Cape's early retirement, which had been put down to him wanting to spend more time with his family during difficult times. Not untrue. Happy campers all round. Which was not what he had originally foreseen when this mess had erupted.

Kate: new job. Cape: retired with his dignity intact—a decision for which Alessandro had not catered but one with which he was pleased. Several members of the accounts team had been reshuffled, much to their individual satisfaction.

Unfortunately *he* didn't feel like a happy camper, and it was getting on his nerves.

He was pinning a lot on the curative powers of Red-Hot Rebecca.

On the spur of the moment he dialled through to Kate's cell phone, wanting to remind himself of what was history. He was branching out in a different direction with a different woman, and from nowhere came the urge to satisfy himself that he was over his brief liaison with Kate. Aside from which he had a couple of things to ask her. Rebecca would be more than happy to wait for five minutes for him downstairs if traffic was light and she arrived sooner than expected. She wasn't the clingy sort who would throw a fit if he was a little late.

Her cell phone was answered immediately.

'It's Alessandro.'

On the other end of the line, Kate felt her heart skip a beat.

There had been no need for him to announce himself. She would have recognized that deep, dark, lazy drawl anywhere. And after nearly two weeks of trying to get it out of her head she found that it still did the same crazy things to her nervous system it had done when they had almost lived in each other's company.

She had done the right thing in ending it. She knew that. He had wanted to carry on until he got bored, but she had noticed that he hadn't put up much of a fight when she had swept past that interruption. Just as she had noticed that he had made no effort to try and contact her since they had arrived back in London.

He had delegated all the work for her hand-over to his financial director. She had got the message loud and clear. If she'd been up for a little more fun and frolics then he would have happily obliged, but the second she had refused he had shrugged, backed away and headed off in the opposite direction. No big deal.

Except for her it was all a big deal. She missed him. She missed everything about him. On paper, it didn't make sense. On paper, the only thing that should have glued them together was the sex. But unfortunately life couldn't be worked out on paper—even though she had spent years trying to make sure that it did.

Unfortunately for her the guy who made no sense was also the guy who had made her ridiculously happy. He was the guy who had bandaged her feet and carried her to that spot where they had had a picnic because he had told her that he didn't want her feet to be aching when they headed back to the bedroom later. He was the guy who had made her laugh, and he had shown her a side of himself that was empathetic and considerate in the way he had dealt with George.

He was also the guy who had refused to discuss anything he considered too personal.

And what did that say? Several times she had tried to talk to him about his childhood, about his parents. After all, he knew all about hers! He might have confided a little, but beyond that *little* there had been no more on the table.

What that said to her was that he was not prepared to take things a step further, and she hated herself for knowing that that was what she had ended up wanting. Ended up *craving*.

Because she had fallen in love with him.

She'd gone and torn up the rule book and done the one thing she had promised herself she *wouldn't* do. In fact she had done the one thing she had been so convinced she wouldn't be in danger of doing because Alessandro Preda and her, as a couple, *made no sense.*

So much for relationships that made sense. Another myth to be chucked out of the window.

At least she hadn't gone running back to him with a change of heart, greedy to take the crumbs that might still be on offer. Not that she hadn't thought about that on more than one occasion. Knocking on his door…telling him that she had thought things over…that he was right…that she wanted to carry on sleeping with him until the fire burnt out…

He wasn't to know that there was no danger of *her* fire burning out, was he?

But she had resisted.

It was only now, when she heard his voice, that she realized just how much she'd ached for him to get in touch with her.

And he had.

She didn't dare contemplate what that meant, but she dared to hope…

She wasn't sure that she would even be able to play it cool. Of course she wouldn't *leap* into immediate acquiescence… She might allow a heartbeat's pause, so that he could understand that she was actually considering turning him away, but then she would crack. She knew she would because the past eleven days had been the worst in her entire life.

'I was just about to leave,' she said, in what she hoped was a cool, calm and collected voice—as opposed to one that sounded breathless, excited, which was how she was feeling. 'I guess you're phoning to talk about the problems with the Wilson deal? Watson Russell told me that you were concerned they were going to pull out at the last minute and that I was to do whatever was in my power to stop that from happening. I'm pleased to say that I think I may have persuaded them to go ahead...'

'The Wilson deal... Yes...of course...'

'I really do think that it's a brilliant direction to go in...electronics and telecommunications might be right up there when it comes to making huge profits, but it's important that we keep publishing companies alive. And this small one, if it's developed and run properly, stands a good chance of making a profit. I told Ralph Wilson all of this, and he seemed very happy.'

'Drop the files up for me,' Alessandro told her abruptly.

'Sure. I'll make sure they're on your desk first thing in the morning.'

'Wrong response. When I said *drop the files*

up for me, I meant bring them to my office—right now.'

Did he want to see her? Hell, why not?

He phoned through to Rebecca, told her to wait for him in Reception…that he had some last-minute business to tie up…and was told, in reply, that there was no rush. She was working on her laptop in the taxi because her working day never seemed to end…blah, blah, blah…

Alessandro barely heard the tail end of her sentence because there was a knock on his door and his whole body tensed in anticipation of seeing Kate…

Which enraged him.

His face revealed nothing, but in the space of a few seconds his cool dark eyes had clocked her from head to toe.

And he didn't like what he saw.

Where the hell had the suit gone? Aside from that little window in time when she had let her hair down she had always worn suits. Grey suits, black suits, navy suits, the daring cream one…

No suit. She was wearing a floaty dress in smoky blue colours over which a businesslike blazer did absolutely nothing to hide the sexy body underneath. And she wasn't wearing pumps. She was wearing sandals. Flat blue sandals with diamanté on the straps. And she had painted her toenails—a pale transluscent pink that matched the polish on her fingernails and also her lip gloss.

'So sorry,' he drawled, turning his back on her and walking towards his desk. 'It appears I've stopped you on your way to a cocktail party...'

Kate reddened and said nothing.

She had hoped for...*what*, exactly? Disappointment raced through her and she could have kicked herself. She had thought...*what?* That he had called her to his office as an excuse to see her?

'Here are the files.'

She held them out and was ignored, although he did signal to his desk, where she dropped them before spinning round, ready to head for the door, mortified at the optimism that had made her re-apply her lip gloss and straighten her hair. Which was tied back but no longer in its severe bun. Instead it was loose, with only two blue clips on either side restraining the riot of tumbling waves.

'Wait a sec...' Alessandro drawled, ignoring the files. 'How are the team settling into their new roles?'

She turned slowly to face him and focused on a spot just beyond his shoulder. Safer. No perilous eye-to-eye contact. 'You should know how they're settling in. It's early days, but I did have a debrief with my new boss... I filled him in on how everyone's adapting to their new roles... Hasn't he reported back to you?'

'I take it from your remarkable shift in dress code that you've vacated the ivory tower…?'

'I don't know what that's supposed to mean.'

'It means that after a lifetime of suits you seem to have adopted a different dress code for work…'

'I've adopted the same dress code as everyone else…' She glanced down at her very respectable outfit, feeling the rake of his dark eyes on her and remembering everything she knew she should be forgetting.

Alessandro saw the buzz of his mobile and ignored it. Red-Hot Rebecca could wait for a couple more minutes.

'And what else has changed…hmm?' he enquired softly.

'I have no idea what you're talking about,' Kate answered tonelessly. 'But if that's all I'll be on my way.'

'On your way where? You never said…'

'Actually, I *do* happen to be going out tonight…' Did the supermarket qualify as 'going out'? she wondered. 'And then I shall be spending the weekend away. So…'

Alessandro clenched his jaw. *Where?* Where was she going later? And with whom? And would it just happen to be the same person she would be spending the weekend with?

Demanding questions surged through his head with angry force, and making him even angrier was the fact that his libido was rising faster than a rocket from a launch pad. That flimsy dress was made to be ripped off. That little line of tiny pearly buttons would challenge any man with the slightest sex drive—and *his* sex drive was unstoppable.

Another buzz on his mobile. He shoved it into his pocket and ignored it.

'Are you going anywhere exciting?' he asked through gritted teeth.

Kate laughed gaily. 'Oh, is there anywhere in London that *isn't* exciting? So many clubs and restaurants! Although I shall be heading out of London for the weekend. It's always nice to have a change of scenery...'

What the hell could he say to *that*?

Hadn't he told her often enough that it was all about fun? All about sex and letting her hair down?

She *had* let her hair down...and who the hell was she having sex with...?

He was spared having to say anything else because just at that moment his office door was pushed open and his date...Red-Hot Rebecca, with the medicinal powers to rescue him from his ongoing foul mood...was stepping into his office.

He forced himself to smile. Rebecca was in red. Red dress barely skimming long white legs...red clutch bag...scarlet lipstick... Red was the one colour Kate always avoided. He remembered her saying so. Some passing titbit of information that had stuck in his head.

The hotshot lawyer was dressed for play—and all of a sudden she was the last thing Alessandro wanted. Why hadn't she waited in Reception?

Kate, positively demure by comparison, still managed to have the sex appeal of a siren, luring him on, making him blind to his date and everything he had hoped she might do for him.

'Kate…this is…Rebecca…' He shot his date a sideways glance before his eyes returned compulsively to Kate, keenly noting the barely there flush that tinged her cheeks.

Something insane and ridiculously childish made him want to sling his arm around Rebecca just to see what reaction that would evoke in Kate, but he resisted the impulse. He was jealous of whoever she was about to see…whoever she was going to be spending the weekend with…and he wanted her to be jealous too…

It felt like an incontrollable weakness.

Kate was already looking at Rebecca, her eyes guarded and unrevealing.

'You must be the finance bod.' Rebecca broke the silence. 'You poor dear… I do hope the brute pays you well for working late…?'

She flashed Alessandro an intimate, raised eyebrows smile that made Kate's teeth snap together.

'Although my sympathies are with *you*, my dear…' she continued in her cut-glass voice. 'I'm about to take silk and working late is something of a habit now…positively dreadful…'

'Dreadful,' Kate agreed dully.

'Alessandro…' The striking brunette turned to Alessandro and coiled her arm into his. 'Shall we let this poor thing get on with the rest of her life…? It's too, *too* naughty of you to keep her here—especially when we should be getting on…'

'We have tickets to the opera,' Alessandro said roughly. 'Although…' he disengaged his arm and stepped to one side, shoving both hands in his pockets '…I'm afraid that might have to be put on the back burner…'

'Why?' Rebecca demanded. A querulous note had crept into her voice.

'Because the file Kate has brought up requires some urgent work…'

'I think I've covered all the tricky bits,' Kate said tightly. 'Please… Don't let me keep you both from…' Words failed her and she took a deep breath. 'From your plans for this evening.' She smiled at Rebecca and cool blue eyes met hers. 'I'm in a bit of a rush as well…' she explained faintly.

'That's as may be… But part and parcel of your new position is a willingness to do overtime when it's necessary. It's necessary *now.*'

Alessandro looked at Rebecca. It had been a major mistake to renew contact with the lawyer. It had been an even bigger mistake to summon Kate to his office. And even worse than both those big mistakes had been the mistake of seeing them both alongside one another—because it had only fuelled his frustration at not having Kate to himself.

Not being able to touch her.

He raked his fingers through his hair, realized that he was shaking—but because of what, exactly, he wasn't sure.

'Apologies.' This to an increasingly annoyed Rebecca. 'My driver will return you to your house—unless you'd like to take someone to the opera with you...'

He was already flipping open his cell, giving instructions to his driver to come to the office.

'Are you telling me that I'm being *stood up*?' Rebecca hissed as she was ushered towards the door. She tugged free of his grasp and spun round to face him, hands on hips. 'Believe me, Alessandro, I have better things to do than to come here and find myself without a date for the evening!'

'Again... I apologize...'

'Not good enough!'

'Unfortunately...' he eased her out of the door '...it will have to do...'

'There was no need to...to do that...' Kate felt

the tiny pulse in her neck beating as she stared at him. 'There's really nothing...nothing that can't wait until next week...to be sorted...'

'You've been in your new role for under two weeks,' said Alessandro, knowing very well that she was right. 'Do me the courtesy of not over-stepping your brief.'

'Your date must have been disappointed.'

'That's very considerate of you... I can't say I'm half as considerate towards yours...'

'Sorry?'

'The clothes...the make-up...the sexy little san-dals—which, I notice, you can now wear *without* a serious onset of blisters. I'm not an idiot, Kate. You might not be on the way to a cocktail party, but you sure as hell won't be having a meal in on your own tonight...'

He swung round and strolled towards the win-dow, trying hard to get his act together.

He turned to face her, back to the window, arms folded. 'You move fast.'

'That's rich, coming from you!' Patches of angry colour stained her cheeks.

How dared he accuse her of moving fast when he was already involved with another woman?

'Who is he anyway?'

'We're no longer an item, Alessandro. My pri-vate life is none of your business now...'

'It is when it involves you playing hanky-panky with a colleague!'

'That's ridiculous. Who am I supposed to be...? To be...?'

'Say it, Kate! Spit it out! *Playing with... Having an affair with... Having sex with...*'

'I would *never* do anything with a work colleague,' she flung back at him.

But she wasn't denying that she was seeing someone...

Maybe not someone she worked with, but nevertheless she was still flaunting herself...parading her femininity where before she had concealed it...

And it was driving him crazy.

He wanted to point out that she was in a position of responsibility, that climbing the career ladder *didn't* involve wearing clothes that turned men on... But where the hell would he be going with that anyway? He wasn't a dinosaur, and there was no rigid dress code within his company aside from the fact that his employees had to look 'smart'.

'You're *jealous*...'

And that angered her—because he had no right to be. Not when he was seeing another woman. Not when he had moved on at the speed of light. *He* had no right to be jealous just because *she* had been the one to walk away.

She felt sick when she thought of him and the lawyer in the short red dress.

She felt sick because he had broken with tradition and was going out with someone smart, someone high-powered, someone with a cut-glass accent—someone just like him.

Alessandro had never been jealous in his life before, but he couldn't contradict her.

'*You've* found someone else,' Kate threw at him, 'but you still can't bear the thought that I was the one who walked away from you, can you?'

He no longer wanted her, but he wasn't quite ready for her to want anyone else.

Was that it? Alessandro thought.

He didn't say anything. Instead he strolled slowly towards her and Kate backed away, as terrified as a rabbit caught in the glare of oncoming headlights.

Terrified because she knew that he could still have her. It was mortifying.

Her breasts felt heavy, as if remembering his touch. Her nipples tightened as she imagined his mouth on them, his tongue licking and teasing them, and between her legs she knew that she was wet for him.

She half closed her eyes, dazed at the graphic memory of him down there, sucking her, taking his time, his big hands on her inner thighs, making sure her legs were open for his lazy exploration. She remembered what it had felt like to gaze down at that dark head between her legs, to have her fingers coiled in his hair as she urged him on.

She bumped into the edge of his desk and didn't even know how she had managed to stumble back there.

'You still want me,' Alessandro growled.

She shook her head in helpless denial but her eyes, pinned to his face, were telling a different story.

He was so hot for her that it hurt. Very slowly he dragged his finger gently along her cheek. She turned her head away sharply. But her breathing was ragged, all over the place, and he could *feel* her body burning up for him.

Kate licked her lips.

'I… I…' Her throat was so dry that she could barely get the words out.

You have a girlfriend…you have a hotshot lawyer… Okay, so you might have dispatched her tonight, but she'll still be hanging around, waiting for you to say the word, because that's just what women do for you… But not me.

'Tell me that you don't…' he murmured roughly. 'Tell me that whoever this guy is…whoever you've picked up…he can make you feel the way I make you feel. Tell me that if I were to slide my fingers into you right now you wouldn't open up for me…'

'No!' Kate pulled away and managed to galvanize her unsteady legs into action. 'You've moved on. I've moved on. Nothing...nothing else matters...'

She couldn't look at him. If she looked at him—looked into those deep, dark eyes—she would be lost.

She fled.

She was so scared he would follow her that she didn't dare look round. Her whole body prickled with tension. Her fingers were trembling as she repeatedly jabbed the button to call the lift. When it finally whirred up she leapt through the doors and pressed herself against the mirrored back, only breathing out when she was disgorged onto the ground floor.

He'd played with her the way a cat played with a mouse—toying with her to prove a point.

He'd proved it.

For the first time ever she had a driving need to talk to her mother—to actually *talk* to her about her feelings.

Nothing had gone according to plan, and that was something Shirley Watson would understand. None of *her* life had gone according to plan. She had lurched from one guy to another in search of love. And she, Kate, had tried so hard to make sure she went in the opposite direction to her mother.

She had formulated her Plan A and had been

determined to stick to it. *Now* look at her! Whatever plan she had ended up on, it certainly wasn't
Plan A. She wasn't even sure it was Plan B.

She dialled her mother's number and burst into
tears at the sound of her mother's voice.

'Mum,' she finally hiccuped, 'I've made such
a mess of things… I've just gone and done the stu-
pidest thing… I've fallen in love with the wrong
man…'

'Oh, Katie. It's not the end of the world…
You're crying, my darling. Please don't cry. You're
such a strong young woman. What can I say? I've
always known that you disapproved of my lifestyle, but it's better to have fallen in love with the
wrong man than to never know what it is to fall
in love. Come down to Cornwall…spend a few
days. Sea air is very good for clearing the head…'

There was no Red-Hot Rebecca spending the night
for fun, games and a future of intellectual stim-
ulation. She had been permanently dispatched.

Alessandro had spent the past hour wandering
from room to room in his enormous house, unable to settle down. Work was no distraction from
his thoughts, and right up there when it came to
those thoughts was: Who the hell was her date
and where the hell was she going to be spending
the weekend?

And hard on the heels of that thought was another disturbing one… Why did he care? Why did it make him feel slightly sick whenever he thought of her with another man?

She still wanted him, but having proved that left him empty. She might burn for him but she had run away…hadn't looked back.

And it wasn't in him to chase a woman. He had never done that and never would. Chasing implied a lack of control, and he only had to look at his parents to see where that led. Their crazy love had resulted in an utter lack of control. They were so similar that they couldn't help but egg each other on in their harebrained antics. For them, the rest of the world didn't really exist—and that was a dangerous place for them to occupy.

That said, he spent the evening on his own, drinking too much and then suffering the after-effects with a sleepless night and a headache that kept him in bed until eight the following morning.

Where could she possibly be going for a week-end with a guy she'd only just met? Was the woman completely off her head? Had she flung herself into some kind of random affair with a man who could turn out to be anybody? Wasn't she aware that that was a dangerous game to play?

And how could she get involved with someone else when she was still wrapped up in him?

He couldn't. He'd tried, but he hadn't been able to.

Kate might think that she was a tough, sassy career woman but she wasn't. Dig a little and what you found was someone who was vulnerable— someone who was waiting to be taken advantage of, someone who wouldn't be able to spot danger if it approached ringing bells and announcing itself through a megaphone.

She had been as safe as houses with him, but who knew what she would find with some man she had probably picked up in a bar somewhere? Because sure as hell she didn't keep a little black book full of useful rainy-day numbers. Whoever this mystery guy was, she would have found him in just the sort of place where predators waited for gullible single girls to appear. A sexy-as-hell single girl would be like manna from heaven.

She might think that she was forging ahead on some new, independent path, but she was too naive to realize that any path that involved sex would be littered with potholes and pitfalls for someone who still believed in fairy tales.

He didn't think twice. He knew where she lived.

What harm was there in just going over? Making sure that she hadn't found herself in some sort of perilous situation she couldn't cope with? Or even some sort of fairly harmless situation she couldn't cope with?

What was the big deal in being a guy who could see the bigger picture? He was magnanimous enough not to be churlish just because she had decided to move on with her life. Even though she still fancied him.

Besides, he was pretty sure he needed to go out to buy something anyway. Coffee… Newspapers…

This would be a multipurpose trip.

CHAPTER TEN

KATE HAD NEVER in a million years thought that her mother could be a source of comfort when it came to the whole big love thing. But Shirley Watson had risen to the occasion and surprised her. She was, as she had said with an uninhibited laugh, the queen of broken hearts.

'But, really, my heart was only broken once,' she had said. 'And that was when your father left. I just needed to find my way via a lot of frogs to realize that I could never replace him. I had to look in different places for a different sort of man. But guess what? Even if I could have turned back time and saved myself the heartache of falling for a guy who would leave me, I would have said no. Because falling for your dad was the best bit of falling I ever did.'

Kate double-checked that everything in the house was as it should be and glanced down at the holdall in which New Kate had been packed. New Kate being the Kate who wore clothes that

suited a girl her age instead of the clothes of someone three times her age.

Unfortunately Old Kate was not managing to
keep pace, and Old Kate was the one who had
fallen in love with the wrong man, who didn't fit
the pretty, carefree outfits, who still wanted to
hide behind her armour of suits and flat shoes and
high-necked blouses and baggy jackets.

She sighed and thought that there was no point
in killing time. It was going to be a long trip—although her mother had told her that she intended
shopping in Exeter, that she would get the train
and meet her there, and then they could continue
the remainder of the journey together. At least she
wouldn't be on the road alone for longer than three
and a half hours, all being kind with the traffic.

It was just as well, because she felt exhausted.

How *could* he have just replaced her with someone else in such a short space of time? And how
could he have done what he had—turned her on,
made her remember what she didn't want to remember?

Speculation took root and had a field day in
her head.

Had Alessandro been seeing the lawyer before
he had decided to indulge in a fling with her?
Maybe they had had an argument. Two high-powered people...that would be fertile ground for all

sorts of arguments. Perhaps their timetables had clashed. Perhaps he had *wanted more*.

Or maybe he had come to his senses and done the comparisons… An employee who believed in love was a waste of energy next to a lawyer who was heading in the same direction he was. They could make appointments to meet up and book dates in bed to accommodate their frantic time-tables. For a man who had no heart that would be the ideal arrangement, and perhaps he had worked that out for himself.

Or maybe…

Maybe it was even simpler than that.

Maybe he had realized that he was way too good for the daughter of a cocktail waitress. The sex had been good…*great*…but it paid to pay attention to the detail, and one big detail was the ease with which he had accepted her decision to end things. If he had wanted her enough he would surely have put up a bit more of a fight… He had just been soothing his ego by proving that she still wanted him. If only he knew…

So, all in all, good riddance!

She pressed on the accelerator of her hire car and a glance at the dashboard showed her that she had been driving for over an hour. She had been operating on autopilot, barely noticing the motor-way whizzing past.

The grey summer skies had finally cleared and

it was a beautiful morning. She turned the radio on, adjusted the channels until she found one that had suitably peppy driving music, and then resigned herself to the remainder of the journey being spent in a state of pointless introspection.

There were only so many distressing scenarios she could play over and over in her head, but she thought that she might quite like to wallow in them.

In fact she was sure that she could add to the tally, and thereby get even more depressed than she already was.

It was a little after one by the time she made it to Exeter, which was thick with traffic on this Saturday afternoon.

She had suggested that her mother live in Exeter when she had planned on making her big move to the coast. She had thought that her mother would find it impossible to live in the middle of nowhere, but she had been wrong.

Not only had her mother loved Cornwall from the very second she'd gone there, but she had thrived.

And for the first time she was realizing that there were other things about her mother she had maybe not quite appreciated.

True, Shirley Watson had flung herself headlong into love after love after love, with the desperation of a starving man trying to grab at food that was always just out of reach, but she had not become embittered.

When it came to parenting Kate had summed her up as fragile, but she had been strong enough to do a pretty good job as it turned out.

She, on the other hand, with all her preparations and her precautions, her wariness and her insistence on being able to control her choices, had been the one to end up making the biggest mistake of all in falling in love with Alessandro.

Kate turned the volume up, crawled through the outskirts of the city and after a lot of hunting, managed to locate a car park.

She'd managed to complete the entire journey without really being aware of her surroundings except to marvel at how light the traffic had been.

Forging her way through the crowded streets, she decided that that was probably because everyone had already descended on the city. It was a tourist hotspot and packed.

When she finally made it to the Cathedral square, she couldn't help but notice all the loved-up young couples lazing in the sunshine.

Some people made smart choices.

She was hot and flustered when she spotted her mother, sitting in front of a glass of wine with a pot of tea next to it, as though the healthy beverage atoned for the slightly less healthy one.

Kate smiled.

Thank goodness she was out of London. The long drive had helped her put a lot into perspective—such as how you could think you knew someone only to find that you didn't...not really. She was looking forward to getting to know her mother a whole lot better.

Over tea or wine or whatever...

Now that he knew where she had gone Alessandro slowed his pace, for the first time really questioning why he had made this trip, why he had followed her like a police officer hot on the trail of a wanted felon. He had arrived to see her driving off, had spotted the pull-along case—the same one she had brought with her to Toronto—and he had seen red.

Part of him had thought that all her talk about having a date and being booked up for the weekend had been nothing but hot air. She just wasn't the type who stepped out of one relationship only to immediately fling herself into another, especially when she still fancied him as much as he still fancied her.

He had been wrong.

God only knew where this sex-fest weekend was going to take place, but he'd intended to find out—and rather than overtake her, force her to pull to the kerb and then demand an answer which she was unlikely to give him, he had decided just to…follow her.

It hadn't been hard.

She had no idea what car he'd be in. He had several cars, and the black Range Rover was a whole lot less conspicuous than the Ferrari. He had made sure to keep a safe distance behind her, but he probably could have been attached to her bumper and she wouldn't have noticed. Who really ever paid attention to other cars on the road unless they were misbehaving?

He'd known from the route she was taking that she was heading for the West Country and he hadn't been able to believe it.

She was going to spend the weekend with a perfect stranger, miles away from her home ground? Who the hell did that?

And now here he was, in a picturesque city square, with quaint Tudor-beamed buildings lining it, standing in front of a coffee shop, for the first time in his life hesitating.

A coffee shop was hardly the raunchy, seedy motel he had been expecting. A coffee shop smacked of a nerd—or some clever smart-ass *pretending* to be a nerd. Someone who didn't make her lose control…someone who wasn't…*him*.

But, having come this far, he had no intention of leaving without first confronting his *rival*.

Because that was what it felt like. Sitting somewhere in that coffee shop was his rival—some man he didn't know from Adam, who was laying claim to his woman. It was a possessive feeling, it was unwelcome and it was…the way it was.

He strode forward.

'Good heavens.'

'What?'

'There's a gentleman by the door…quite arresting…'

Kate had had her fill of 'arresting' men. She had come to the conclusion that they all spelt bad news. She wasn't interested—and besides, she was too busy getting rid of her misery via the plate of cakes that had been put between them. Her mother had nibbled one. She was on her fourth. Not only was she destined to be a spinster, she would end up being a fat spinster.

'He's coming over here…'

If she had never agreed to go to Toronto with him she wouldn't be sitting here now, stacking on the pounds and fighting off a crying jag. If she hadn't be so arrogant as to think that she could control the situation—could sleep with him and still hang on to her heart—she wouldn't be here. There were so many steps along the way that could have saved her from being where she was now that she felt giddy when she thought about them.

She was lost in her thoughts, and when she heard that deep, sexy drawl she immediately put it down to the fact that she was probably hallucinating.

Except her mother was still staring, the voice had said something else and the young waitress who had been walking towards them had stopped and her jaw had dropped.

Heart beating fast, Kate slowly twisted round and there he was—larger than life and just as devastating.

Staring down at her, his dark eyes unfathomable.

'You played fast and loose with the speed limit on the motorway,' Alessandro murmured, instantly clocking the situation and feeling lightheaded with relief because *this* was her weekend date.

There was little doubt that the older and still stunningly attractive woman staring at him, openmouthed, was her mother.

'I'm Alessandro, by the way...' He turned to the blonde, hand outstretched. 'I'm guessing you must be Kate's mother...'

'What are you doing here?'

Kate found her voice at last and anger surged up through her—anger that he had the barefaced cheek to have landed himself here when she was on the verge of congratulating herself on having

put some temporary distance between them…
anger that her whole body had lit up like tinder
in receipt of a life-giving flame…anger that none
of the bracing little homilies she had given herself
on the drive down counted for anything when he
was standing right here in front of her…anger at
the power he had over her…

Had he come here for a repeat performance of
proving just how much he could affect her?

'Why are you *here*?'

'Darling, I shall leave you two to get on with
things. I have a bit more shopping to do, as a matter of fact.'

Shirley Watson was already standing and reach-
ing for her handbag, ignoring the desperate yelp
coming from her daughter.

'Shoes…' She addressed Alessandro. 'A girl's
best friend… I've tried my entire life to instil that
into my beautiful daughter, but I see that it actually took you to succeed…'

Kate watched in horror as her mother—*her
treacherous and disloyal mother*—disappeared
with a cheery wave, leaving her seat vacant for
Alessandro to sit on.

Which he did. Not once taking his eyes from
her face.

'How *dare* you follow me? What were you
thinking? I can't *believe* you followed me here!'

'I was worried.'

'You were *worried?* What's *that* supposed to mean?'

She couldn't peel her eyes from his face. God, he was handsome. A little drawn, perhaps, a bit haggard, but even drawn and haggard he was still drop-dead gorgeous.

'You just took off.' Alessandro loathed the defensive note that had crept into his voice. 'On a so-called *weekend away.* I assumed——'

'Oh, I get it,' Kate said with blistering resentment. 'You decided that I was going to meet some man, and also decided that I was too incompetent to look after myself. Or maybe you thought that I didn't dare meet up with anyone because there's a bit of you still in my system...?'

'What was I supposed to think when you refused to tell me where you were going?' So she had admitted it—and it thrilled him.

'I didn't *refuse* to tell you anything! I assumed that it was none of your business! And what would your lawyer girlfriend say if she knew you were here?'

It took him a couple of seconds to comprehend what she was talking about, and a few more seconds to bypass the instinctive clamp-down on explaining himself—which was something he never did. 'There's no connection there...'

'Oh, right. You mean you slept with her and then decided that she didn't fit the bill after all?'

She hated the weakness that was driving her to find out whether he and the lawyer had ended up in bed. It didn't matter! What mattered was that he had rushed down here in her wake because he had some stupid, over-developed he-man instinct to make sure she wasn't going to do anything crazy. Like actually get a life.

'We never made it to the bedroom,' Alessandro admitted in a driven voice.

That stopped Kate in her tracks. It wasn't just what he had said, it was *how* he had said it—it was the way he was pointedly not looking at her, the way he had flung himself back in the chair and was staring around him as though fascinated by his surroundings.

'Well, it doesn't matter anyway.'

'This is not the place for this conversation.'

'It's *exactly* the place for this conversation!' She breathed deeply and then sighed. 'Look, I don't need this. What we had is over. Finished. I just need you to get out of my life—and if you can't do that then I'm going to have to hand in my resignation.'

'It's not finished,' Alessandro muttered in a low, unsteady voice.

He leaned towards her. He was a man with one foot dangling over the side of a cliff and he knew he was going to jump and damn the consequences.

'Not for me. Please, Kate. Let's go somewhere—anywhere. It's too small here...too packed...too mundane and busy for what I have to say...'

'Which is *what*? No, let me guess! You want me back so that you can have a little more *fun* before I end up next to the lawyer who never made it past first base before boring you...'

'Something...happened...'

'Yes, I know what happened,' Kate intoned bitterly. 'You couldn't stand the thought of me walking away from you, so you decided to prove to me that I still wanted you. That's why you summoned me to your office, isn't it? So that you could play with me?'

'I summoned you because I...I needed to see you...'

Needed to see me to prove a point.

'You're just so arrogant that you didn't see why you should let me get on with my life. It didn't matter that you were busy getting on with yours. As far as you were concerned, I didn't *have* a life to get on with because I still felt something for you. You just couldn't accept that I wasn't interested in carrying on with a fling that wasn't going anywhere, because in your world the only thing that matters is sex.'

'I wasn't getting on with my life,' Alessandro muttered under his breath.

There was no guidebook when it came to this

kind of conversation, but he was still condemned to have it... Because she just mattered so damn much...

'I tried,' he continued. 'But I couldn't. And I couldn't because something happened when we were in Toronto...'

'Something *happened*...?'

'I never meant to...to get involved...'

He raked his fingers through his hair and his hand was not as steady as it should have been.

'Let's get out of here...please—' He broke off gruffly and, without giving her the chance to lodge another protest, signalled across to the waitress and asked for the bill. 'And you can stop fishing around for money, Kate,' he grated. *'I'm getting this.'*

'Well?'

This when they were outside, heading towards the grass, joining the milling crowds of couples who had made smart choices. She turned to him, shading her eyes from the glare of the sun, and he just looked at her.

'Come on.'

He reached out, clasped her hand, and her whole body quivered. The feel of his fingers linked with hers was like an electric charge, and under its impact her brain shut down. All those protesting voices were silenced as they found a shady spot close to the Cathedral and sat on the ground.

'Just say what you've come to say, Alessandro, and don't bother dressing it up with words you don't mean. You didn't get *involved* with me... not in the way that most people think of involvement. You *sexually connected* with me and you weren't ready for it to end. You couldn't produce proper involvement out of a hat, but you still had to show me that it wasn't over...'

She hugged her knees up to her chest, suddenly drained.

'How was I to know the difference between involvement and a sexual connection?' he said, half to himself. 'How was I supposed to recognize the difference when I had never been presented with the situation before in my life? When we returned to London I figured that I could put you behind me by dipping into someone else...'

'That's just *horrible*.'

'I'm being as honest as I can. It's what I've always done. I've gone from woman to woman, never realizing that the time might come when I would find myself incapable of doing it...'

'You're doing it again, Alessandro,' Kate whispered. 'You're confusing me with words.'

'I'm using words to tell you how I feel... You asked me why I followed you. Well, I followed you because...because I couldn't stand the thought of you touching another man, seeing another man, laughing with another man...'

'You were only jealous because you weren't ready for me to let you go—you would have seen any man as competition—but that's not real jealousy. Real jealousy has its basis in something bigger…stronger… It's different.'

But hope flared…

'In my world there was never a place for jealousy of any kind. It's not an emotion I've ever experienced. But I…I recognized it…' He smiled crookedly. 'And you're right. Real jealousy *does* have its basis in something bigger—much, much bigger than lust. It wasn't just imagining you getting into bed with another man…'

He clenched his jaw and shook away the violence of emotion that assailed him when he thought about that.

'What I felt… I couldn't even bear the thought of you looking at anyone else…talking to anyone else…'

He risked grazing her cheek with his finger. It was enough to send his libido soaring into overdrive and he wanted nothing so much as to take her hand and place it firmly on his erection, so that she could feel what she did to him. He wondered whether she was feeling it too…the current zipping between them, electric and impossibly alive.

'I'd never planned to… God, Kate, you have no idea how much I want you right now…'

'Wanting just isn't enough for me,' she whispered, and a wave of misery threatened to engulf the fragile shoots of hope that had been growing.

'And it's not enough for me either...'

He tilted her face so that she was gazing at him, locking her in their own private world even though they were surrounded by people.

'I never planned on losing control of my emotions,' he told her seriously. 'I've seen what that can do. I watched my parents get lost in each other and I lived through the ramifications. I thought that it was just about money...' He hesitated.

'But it wasn't, was it?' Kate said softly. 'It was more than just having feckless parents who encouraged each other to blow their respective fortunes, who had no self-control... It was about being shoved aside, wasn't it?'

'They were very good at employing nannies. My parents were so wrapped up in one another that they had no time for a kid. No time for anything. I resolved never to let myself succumb to that kind of emotional excess—and, for me, falling in love with a woman constituted that kind of emotional excess...'

Kate found breathing difficult. She feared that if she exhaled she would somehow blow apart the atmosphere.

'But I fell in love, my darling... I didn't plan to, and I don't know when it happened... I just know that when you walked out on me my world stopped turning…'

'You hurt me. I know I walked away, but I still waited for you to come—waited for you to just… *miss me* so much that you couldn't help yourself. I waited for you to catch up with me, and how I felt about you, but then there was that woman in your office and suddenly it was like my whole stupid world really and truly fell apart.'

'I thought I could find myself some clever woman who would give me an uncomplicated life…with none of the inconvenient loss of self-control that came with you. It was a knee-jerk reaction. You had me wrapped around your little finger and I knew that the second I saw you in that dress. God, you have no idea what that did to me…'

'I love you,' Kate said simply. 'I fell in love with you and I knew I had to walk away because I would just end up getting more and more hurt. You couldn't commit and I couldn't settle for anything else.'

'You love me?' Alessandro said shakily, enjoying this loss of self-control with the woman he had given his heart to. 'I guess your mother is going to be in for the surprise of her life, then, isn't she?'

Kate chuckled, delirious with happiness, sliding close to him and knowing that he was as aroused as she at their physical contact. 'I think that she's already had the surprise of her life—when I confided in her, when I stopped pretending to be an emotional robot and showed her that I was human and fallible and an idiot…'

'And how do you think she'll react when we tell her that we're going to be married? Because I can't imagine my life without you, Kate. So… will you marry me? Be my wife? Never leave my side? Have lots of babies for me?'

Would she marry him? Try stopping her!

'Wild horses couldn't stop me!' She laughed and flung her arms around him.

Who said that fairy tales couldn't come true?

* * * * *

LARGER-PRINT BOOKS!
GET 2 FREE LARGER-PRINT NOVELS PLUS
2 FREE GIFTS!

HARLEQUIN®

Romance

From the Heart, For the Heart

YES! Please send me 2 FREE LARGER-PRINT Harlequin® Romance novels and my 2 FREE gifts (gifts are worth about $10). After receiving them, if I don't wish to receive any more books, I can return the shipping statement marked "cancel." If I don't cancel, I will receive 4 brand-new novels every month and be billed just $5.09 per book in the U.S. or $5.49 per book in Canada. That's a savings of at least 15% off the cover price! It's quite a bargain! Shipping and handling is just 50¢ per book in the U.S. and 75¢ per book in Canada.* I understand that accepting the 2 free books and gifts places me under no obligation to buy anything. I can always return a shipment and cancel at any time. Even if I never buy another book, the two free books and gifts are mine to keep forever.

119/319 HDN GHWC

Name _____ (PLEASE PRINT) _____

Address _____ Apt. # _____

City _____ State/Prov. _____ Zip/Postal Code _____

Signature (if under 18, a parent or guardian must sign)

Mail to the Reader Service:
IN U.S.A.: P.O. Box 1867, Buffalo, NY 14240-1867
IN CANADA: P.O. Box 609, Fort Erie, Ontario L2A 5X3
Want to try two free books from another line?
Call 1-800-873-8635 or visit www.ReaderService.com.

* Terms and prices subject to change without notice. Prices do not include applicable taxes. Sales tax applicable in N.Y. Canadian residents will be charged applicable taxes. Offer not valid in Quebec. This offer is limited to one order per household. Not valid for current subscribers to Harlequin Romance Larger-Print books. All orders subject to credit approval. Credit or debit balances in a customer's account(s) may be offset by any other outstanding balance owed by or to the customer. Please allow 4 to 6 weeks for delivery. Offer available while quantities last.

Your Privacy—The Reader Service is committed to protecting your privacy. Our Privacy Policy is available online at www.ReaderService.com or upon request from the Reader Service.

We make a portion of our mailing list available to reputable third parties that offer products we believe may interest you. If you prefer that we not exchange your name with third parties, or if you wish to clarify or modify your communication preferences, please visit us at www.ReaderService.com/consumerschoice or write to us at Reader Service Preference Service, P.O. Box 9062, Buffalo, NY 14240-9062. Include your complete name and address.

HRLP15

LARGER-PRINT BOOKS!
GET 2 FREE LARGER-PRINT NOVELS PLUS
2 FREE GIFTS!

HARLEQUIN®

super romance®

More Story...More Romance

YES! Please send me 2 FREE LARGER-PRINT Harlequin® Superromance® novels and my 2 FREE gifts (gifts are worth about $10). After receiving them, if I don't wish to receive any more books, I can return the shipping statement marked "cancel." If I don't cancel, I will receive 4 brand-new novels every month and be billed just $5.94 per book in the U.S. or $6.24 per book in Canada. That's a savings of at least 12% off the cover price! It's quite a bargain! Shipping and handling is just 50¢ per book in the U.S. or 75¢ per book in Canada.* I understand that accepting the 2 free books and gifts places me under no obligation to buy anything. I can always return a shipment and cancel at any time. Even if I never buy another book, the two free books and gifts are mine to keep forever.

132/332 HDN GHVC

Name	(PLEASE PRINT)	

Address		Apt. #

City	State/Prov.	Zip/Postal Code

Signature (if under 18, a parent or guardian must sign)

Mail to the **Reader Service:**
IN U.S.A.: P.O. Box 1867, Buffalo, NY 14240-1867
IN CANADA: P.O. Box 609, Fort Erie, Ontario L2A 5X3

Want to try two free books from another line?
Call 1-800-873-8635 today or visit www.ReaderService.com.

* Terms and prices subject to change without notice. Prices do not include applicable taxes. Sales tax applicable in N.Y. Canadian residents will be charged applicable taxes. Offer not valid in Quebec. This offer is limited to one order per household. Not valid for current subscribers to Harlequin Superromance Larger-Print books. All orders subject to credit approval. Credit or debit balances in a customer's account(s) may be offset by any other outstanding balance owed by or to the customer. Please allow 4 to 6 weeks for delivery. Offer available while quantities last.

Your Privacy—The Reader Service is committed to protecting your privacy. Our Privacy Policy is available online at www.ReaderService.com or upon request from the Reader Service.

We make a portion of our mailing list available to reputable third parties that offer products we believe may interest you. If you prefer that we not exchange your name with third parties, or if you wish to clarify or modify your communication preferences, please visit us at www.ReaderService.com/consumerchoice or write to us at Reader Service Preference Service, P.O. Box 9062, Buffalo, NY 14240-9062. Include your complete name and address.

"Now here's the strategic difference between us," Alessandro drawled softly. **"I haven't abandoned having fun in favor of some never-never dream of perfection that won't be happening."**

"I haven't done that!"

"No? So when was the last time you had sex?"

Kate's heart was beating so hard that she could almost hear it. When she opened her mouth, the professional with an agenda not to be affected by him had vanished.

"I... Well..."

"When was the last time you just *let go*, Kate? Here's what I'm thinking...that tonight was probably the first time in years that you went out in something other than the sort of clothes someone's great-aunt would be proud to be seen in..."

"That's not fair," she whispered, stung because it was true—horribly, mortifyingly *true*.

"It may not be *nice*, but it's true. When was the last time you felt anything but a need to work and prove yourself? It's a dry life."

"It's..."

"Dry, sterile... You're hiding away from emotion, waiting for the Big Thing to happen, and in the meantime life's passing you by."

"It's not all about sex..."

He didn't answer. He didn't have to. She could read the intent in his eyes and she knew that he was going to kiss her, and she wanted him to. She wanted him to with every fiber of her sex-starved being...even if it made no sense.

Cathy Williams can remember reading Harlequin® books as a teenager, and now that she is writing them, she remains an avid fan. For her, there is nothing like creating romantic stories and engaging plots, and each and every book is a new adventure. Cathy lives in London, and her three daughters, Charlotte, Olivia and Emma, have always been, and continue to be, the greatest inspiration in her life.

Books by Cathy Williams

Harlequin Presents

The Real Romero
The Uncompromising Italian
The Argentinian's Demand
Secrets of a Ruthless Tycoon
Enthralled by Moretti
His Temporary Mistress
A Deal with Di Capua
The Secret Casella Baby
The Notorious Gabriel Diaz
A Tempestuous Temptation

Seven Sexy Sins
To Sin with the Tycoon

Protecting His Legacy
The Secret Sinclair

Visit the Author Profile page
at Harlequin.com for more titles.